PRAIS ... **KATIE MacALISTER**

Memoirs of a Dragon Hunter

"Bursting with the author's trademark zany humor and spicy romance . . . this quick tale will delight paranormal romance fans."—*Publishers Weekly*

Sparks Fly

"Balanced by a well-organized plot and MacAlister's trademark humor."—*Publishers Weekly*

It's All Greek to Me

"A fun and sexy read."—The Season for Romance

"A wonderful lighthearted romantic romp as a kick-butt American Amazon and a hunky Greek find love. Filled with humor, fans will laugh with the zaniness of Harry meets Yacky."—*Midwest Book Review*

Much Ado About Vampires

"A humorous take on the dark and demonic."—*USA Today*

"Once again this author has done a wonderful job. I was sucked into the world of Dark Ones right from the start and was taken on a fantastic ride. This book is full of witty dialogue and great romance, making it one that should not be missed."—Fresh Fiction

The Unbearable Lightness of Dragons

"Had me laughing out loud. . . . This book is full of humor and romance, keeping the reader entertained all the way through . . . a wondrous story full of magic. . . . I cannot wait to see what happens next in the lives of the dragons."—Fresh Fiction

Also By Katie MacAlister

DESPERATELY SEEKING VAMPIRE

A DARK ONES NOVELLA

KATIE MACALISTER

FAT CAT BOOKS

To my darling Michelle, agent extraordinaire, who wanted me to write a small town vampire story.

KATIE'S CLUES FOR THE ... WELL, CONFUSED

Because I know some readers are going to be confused about where in the Dark Ones series this novella falls, I thought I'd give a little info so that we're all on the same page (so to speak).

And because I love bulleted lists—and also, no one uses bulleted lists in notes to readers, and I strive to be eccentric whenever possible—I'm putting the clarifying information in a handy-to-read list.

Ready? Excellent!

- This novella is technically a prequel. That is, the action occurs before the events depicted in *A Girl's Guide to Vampires*, which was published in 2003. Yes, I feel old after looking up that original publication date.
- This means that *Desperately Seeking Vampire* takes place in the autumn of 2002. The Christian Dante you see here has not yet met Joy, Roxy, or his Beloved, Allie. He's just a lonely vampire knocking around a big ole castle, waiting to meet the woman who will bring him to his knees in gratitude. And a lot of frustration, but that story is told in *Sex and the Single Vampire*.

- Yes, I wrote the character of Christian just for me. But I'm willing to share him.
- So, when you are looking at the big list of Dark Ones books (which you can see at https://katiemacalister.com/bookshelf/dark-ones/), *Desperately Seeking Vampire* is Book 0 (that is, it slots in before Book 1).
- Now that we have that taken care of, I know some people are going to squint at the name of the hero of this novella, Ivo. It's pronounced EE-voh. Just think of it as a Latinized version of Yves (which is what it is).
- The poetry that Ivo spouts in this story is written by me, for him. Yes, I deliberately made it horrible.
- The tarot readings in this book were real in that I actually did the tarot card readings you see mentioned in the book. I did not manipulate the outcome at all; I simply drew cards whenever it was called for, and added them into the book with my interpretations. As a big devotee of tarot cards, I had great fun doing readings for the characters.
- Christian's nephew Finch has his own book due out in late 2022.

I hope that takes care of all the possibly confusing points. If there's something that's still puzzling you, drop me an email and let me know.

Onward!

Katie Mac

ONE

Christian Dante
Drahanská Castle
2 July 1916

Uncle Christian,

I have no heart to tell you of the events of today. It seems as if everyone is gone, blood soaking the earth beneath smoking skies. I know that you as well as my father have witnessed many wars between mortals, but this … this is insanity. Rabid dogs set upon each other could not be worse than the atrocities I've seen committed on this day.

If I could escape this hell on earth, I would, but I promised my sainted mother that I would always aid those in need, and I will not risk disturbing her spirit because I left the mortals to massacre themselves.

Do you remember Ivo Zeman? I met him some twenty years ago when we were both in Heidelberg. He has been here at the Somme in the VII Corps for the last two weeks, also as a doctor. He seems to have more of an affinity to it than me, but nonetheless, both his unit and mine have been patching up the shattered remains of mortals as best we could. Then, yesterday, the Germans decimated the British and French ranks. I won't go into details other than to say that Ivo was caught in the middle of it, and wounded grievously.

Naturally, I couldn't tell the other doctors at the regimental aid post or the dressing station that he would recover, given time (and blood). I've done what I can to guard him from too much attention, but a fresh corps of nurses have just arrived from England and Australia. Martinson, the medical officer, has agreed to allow me to attend Ivo since I told him we are old friends. If I can't find someone from whom Ivo can feed tonight, I will let him feed from me. It is not an ideal solution, since I have to go several days between feedings, myself, but such is the situation.

I wish I had better news for my weekly letter, but there is nothing here but suffering, blood, and chaos.

Yours,
Finch

Royal Army Medical Corps, 8th Division
Lieutenant F. T. Dante
France

My dear Finch—I am, naturally, distressed that you are seeing more action than anyone could desire. Were your father still alive, he would be very proud—as am I—that you are remaining to provide what aid you can, despite your desire to be well away from the affairs of mortals.

As for your friend Ivo, did you not bring him to the castle around 1912? I have a memory of Tobar telling me that your mother was worried about the influence of a student who was encouraging you, cognizant that you need not find a Beloved, to cut a swath through the local female population. If this is not the same friend, then I apologize; regardless, I hope he recovers without attracting attention from others. If you have not yet done so, you might try to remove him from the dressing station to your own digs to keep him from garnering too much attention.

I am sending a package containing such supplies as I hope will provide you and your friend with some comfort—books, a gramophone, cigarettes and chocolate for you to pass out amongst the mortals, and several pairs of socks and underclothing. Please let me know if there is anything else you and Ivo can use.

Your devoted uncle,
C. J. Dante

Christian Dante
Drahanská Castle
18 July 1916

Uncle Christian,

Things have gone from bad to worse for Ivo. The day following his injury, I was called out to help at the main trench with the MO. Somehow, Ivo fed. Normally, this would not be a bad thing unless he was caught in the act, but apparently, he fed from one of the field nurses whom the MO had asked to check on him since I was at the front. Ivo doesn't know which one, as he was mostly insensible, having lost a great deal of blood due to the explosion, but he claims he had a dream in which a woman was tending to the wounds, and the next thing he knew, he was feeding from her.

We could probably hush up any complaint the nurse made about him, should she do so, but the situation is much more dire. Although he claims he wasn't aware of it at the time—and given the extreme damage the mortar fire did to him, it is understandable that he was not aware of his surroundings while his body was focused on healing—the woman he fed from was actually his Beloved. He had no sense of her being such, and thus didn't identify himself to her. In fact, he said that as soon as he fed, he fell into an unconscious state, and when he next awoke, different nurses were present. The best description he can give is that she had dark copper red hair, wore spectacles, and was possibly American—Ivo can't remember any distinct accent, but thought she might be American. I don't see how she could be, since the States have thus far refused to join us, but that is what Ivo has told me.

This would be nothing but an interesting side note except now Ivo can't take any blood; evidently it all is as poison to him. I tried feeding him myself despite the fact that hunger gnawing at my vitals has been my constant companion, but he could not tolerate even that.

He has regained enough health that I was able to move him to my tent in order to keep his accelerated healing prowess from attracting notice, but I fear that if we do not locate this nurse who has bound his life to hers, he may perish of starvation. I hate to involve you in my troubles, but I have little time to devote to Ivo with the onslaught of injured and dying men, and he is weak and racked with hunger.

Finch

Royal Army Medical Corps, 8th Division
Lieutenant F. T. Dante
France

My dearest Finch,

The situation is not as dire as you might believe from seeing your friend suffer. While Dark Ones can be killed, as we both know to our sorrow, it is not easy for us to die of hunger. I will do what I can from here to locate all the field nurses in your area, but I fear your attention to this detail will have more potential for success. Turn your efforts—in your free time—to locating the woman. Until such time as you find her, Ivo may find relief for his hunger in whatever animals he can access. I will not detail the many times I was unable to find human sources and had to resort to horses, cattle, and, in particularly distressing times that I do not care to recall, vermin, but nonetheless, all are viable sources when others are not available.

Do not hesitate to tell me if there is anything else I can do. Although I don't hold with mortal religion, I have ordered the local priest to light candles not only for the spirits of your father and mother, but for you and Ivo, as well. Stay safe, and do not lose hope. Beloveds may be rare, but I'm told they have a way of finding their Dark One when all hope is gone.

Your devoted uncle,
C. J. Dante

Christian Dante
Drahanská Castle
1 August 1916

Uncle Christian,

The last three weeks have been a blur of blood, death, and incompetence. Our hospitals are naught more than charnel houses of pain and misery, filled with a daily influx of fresh inmates, but of that, I will refrain from detailing. Suffice it to say that the package you sent, which arrived last week, was most heartily greeted by Ivo, myself, and the men in my division.

Ivo continues, although he is gaunt and weak. I will draw a veil over the sources of his nourishment, as they are of the rodent variety. Since the horses are as overworked and underfed as the rest of the mortals, neither Ivo nor I have the heart to feed from them. I've managed to slip into a nearby town on those occasions when the hunger has become a detriment to doing my job, but other than that, our surroundings, work, and life in general are a never-ending hellscape.

I have managed to steal a list of personnel who were present at the dressing station when Ivo arrived. As you can see, there are fourteen field nurses listed. Most are from Queen Alexandra's Imperial Military Nursing Service, but there are also a handful from the Australian Army Nursing Service. None are American, as I fully expected. Of those fourteen, I've met with nine, none of whom manifested any signs of being a Beloved. A tenth one was sent to a casualty clearing station with pneumonia right after Ivo was injured, so she could not be the woman we seek. I have not yet been able to locate the four remaining women noted on the list—

the Australians were moved shortly after Ivo's wounding to regiments of their countrymen, and the two others sent to a nearby field hospital. If you could use your resources to examine them for signs of rampant Belovedhood, I would be grateful.

Finch

Royal Army Medical Corps, 8th Division
Lieutenant F. T. Dante
France

My dear Finch,

I have done what I could to track down the women you think might be your friend's Beloved. Of them, the two British nurses were cleared by me personally. The remaining two Australians were located near Paris, and were checked by my friend Sebastian, but he said they were not Beloveds. Might the woman in question not have been a nurse? I understand that civilians in that area provide what help they can to the armed forces, and it occurred to me that some such woman, seeing Ivo injured, may have attempted to help him and, in doing so, allowed him to feed from her.

Please press Ivo for what details he can reclaim. I don't relish attempting to interview every woman of a suitable age in the area surrounding the front, but naturally, I will do what I can. If you can get Ivo to remember any more information, I assure you I will put it to the best of use.

Your devoted uncle,

C. J. Dante

Christian Dante
Drahanská Castle
15 September 1916

Uncle: I fear for Ivo. He has not been able to eat in over three weeks. He talks of falling into some sort of death sleep. I am at my wit's end as to what I can do for him. His mental state is fading along with his general health. I've repeatedly asked him for more information about the woman from his "dream," but he has nothing more to add. He talks of nothing but death now, having given up all hope. Considering the stupidity of the battles around us, and the death and destruction that fill our days, I have lost hope, myself.

I don't know what aid you can render us, but if there is anything you can think of, any way for us to locate this woman, please tell me. I am not one to give in to emotion, but I dislike seeing my friends fade away.

Finch

2 October

My dear nephew:

Expect transport for Ivo to arrive as soon as I can receive clearance for the ambulance, hopefully shortly after you receive this note, which I have sent by messenger so that you might receive it promptly.

Did your father never tell you of noctambul? It is the state of, for lack of a better phrase, suspended animation. All Dark Ones can enter noctambul, but it must be conducted at a safe location where protection can be provided for as long as is needed. I will have one of the crypts at Drahanská cleared for Ivo until such time as we can locate his Beloved.

Until that time, assure him that he can rest safely.

Yours in haste,

C. J. Dante

TWO
OCTOBER 2002

"You have got to be crazy!" I slapped my hands down on the police counter, so frustrated I wanted to scream. Or pull out my hair. Or even bang my forehead on said counter, but since none of that would help, I stared in impotent anger at the man who pursed his lips and raised his eyebrows at the same time he gestured toward my bag.

"Here are your things," Andreas the policeman told me in Czech. "You will not yell at me as if I am the thief who stole from all those musicians. I am doing my job, that is all."

"Well, I didn't steal the festival's money, either," I said, contemplating the wisdom of slapping my hand on the counter again. I decided to go with the axiom about sugar being more effective than vinegar, and softened my voice, managing even to summon a smile. "Look, I know this isn't your fault any more than it is mine. Jason is my boss, that's all. I'm just the interpreter making sure that all the bands who've gathered here know what they're doing. I'm a grunt, a nobody." I bit back the urge to add, "... like you."

"It is out of my hands," Andreas said, and pushed my bag at me. "Your passport cannot be returned until such time as we have cleared you of complicity."

"Just because I work for Jason doesn't mean I'm responsible for his actions," I argued.

"You were traveling with him," Andreas said. "And he had possession of your items."

"That's because he sent me to Prague while he was held up in Paris, and it made sense for him to take charge of the luggage. Once I made sure that all the merchandise was packed on the trucks in good order, and was on its way, I came out to Brno pronto. And boom. You guys were waiting for me at the train station. I didn't know you were going to confiscate everything I owned including the money I had on me, and my passport."

"This is what your documentation shows, yes," he agreed, and I had a moment of hope that whatever nefarious activity Jason was up to wouldn't affect me in the end. "With regards to your passport, please note that should you attempt to leave the country before our investigation is finished, you will be detained."

"I have no intention of running away. For one, I've done nothing wrong. And for another, I want my stuff back. Speaking of which, what about my money?" I asked, digging through my bag until I found my wallet, which was empty of both credit cards and cash. "That was my personal money and my personal credit cards, not part of the festival funds that Jason embezzled."

"Ah, but we do not know yet what is what," Andreas said, just as if he was pronouncing something of great wisdom.

I realized that there was no way I was going to convince him to give me back my money. The local police who had nabbed Jason had grilled me for four hours about my involvement with Jason Amiri Sensations and, more importantly, how Jason was caught at the airport with a one-way ticket out of the Czech Republic, leaving the bands, the festival suppliers, and the traveling-circus host holding the (empty) bag. I switched my tactic again. "How am I supposed to pay for food and lodging? With you guys holding Jason in jail, I have to make sure that the battle of the bands goes off OK, and I can't do that if I'm starving and sleep-deprived because you won't even give me one of my credit cards. Just one will do. I'll tell you which one has the lowest credit limit, if that would help."

"You expected to stay here without arranging for a hotel room?" Andreas shook his head before I had finished.

"Jason arranged for that, assumedly using his credit card," I said, more than a little desperate. "I have no idea if the hotel will honor either the reservation or the method of payment. I can't see how you can consider my personal cash and cards as being tied to him just because I work for him."

"It is all evidence until the detectives can verify your information. You will be contacted at that time," he insisted, driving my frustration level sky-high.

"Right. Let's just see what the fates have to say about that." I pulled out a somewhat wrinkled piece of red silk with gold embroidered suns, and unwrapped it to reveal a deck of battered tarot cards.

"You play cards now?" Andreas asked, looking mildly scandalized as I shuffled the cards.

"No. I'm a cartomancer." He blinked at me, and I wondered if I'd used the wrong word. Czech wasn't one of my stronger languages. "I read information in cards, you know?"

"Fortune-teller?" he asked, looking even more scandalized. I had a feeling he wanted to back away from me, but only his training kept him standing attentively at the reception counter.

"Sometimes the cards can give me insight into the future, but mostly, it's just what life wants me to know at that moment. I pull three cards, and see what they tell me."

I turned over three cards, and made a face.

"That looks painful," he said, pointing to the first card.

"It's not as bad as it looks," I said, glaring at the ten of swords. "It basically means that I've hit rock bottom, but that the only way is up. It also tells me that I need to accept a situation giving me grief in order to move forward."

He looked pointedly at me.

"Yeah, yeah, I know."

"What do the others say?" he asked, craning to see them.

"This is the Priestess. She tells me that I need to look within and listen to my own thoughts rather than those of others."

"She is smart," Andreas said, nodding. "And that one?"

"Seven of cups. It means I've been trying to do too many things, and I need to focus on one goal and, in the process, stay connected to what I really want. Which is my passport and money, in case you were wondering," I said, hoping against hope.

He shook his head, and pointed at the Priestess card. "The lady, she says you need to talk to yourself and not others. I am others."

"Sadly," I told him as I gathered up my cards and slid them into their wrap, "that is all too true. Please pass along my request to the detectives investigating my boss that they hurry up with the return of my stuff, or else I'll have to throw myself on the mercy of the Canadian embassy."

He waggled his hand and turned to greet a woman who entered the police station.

I went outside, rubbing my arms against the chill wind. There was simply no other choice—I could make a scene and find myself thrown into a cell next to Jason, or I could gather my dignity and pray that the local police were swift in determining my innocence.

"At least I have my emergency five hundred Czech crowns," I said softly to myself, pulling a tampon out of my bag, and carefully spreading the cottony inner fibers to reveal the bill I'd tucked away in case my wallet was stolen. I clutched the money—worth a little more than twenty dollars—as I glanced around nervously. I debated spending some of its precious amount to get out to the north pasture where GothFaire was hosting the Harvest Festival Battle of the Bands, and decided, with a martyred sigh, that I would survive the chilly three-mile walk.

To say the festival was pandemonium would be understating the level of chaotic energy that all but made the air crackle with electricity.

"What's going to happen to the contest?" The questions pelted me as soon as I arrived at the outskirts of the temporary stage. "Is it true the organizer skipped out with the prize money? Are we not going to be able to play?"

The questions went on and on for a good four minutes in a variety of languages. I let everyone have their say before I held up my hands, climbed onto a portable picnic table, and announced, "Guys, the police have Jason Amiri in the local jail. They also have the prize money, which they said they will release in the next couple of days, pending investigation. I've given them the information about the festival, Jason's role in organizing it, and provided them with all the details I had in my possession. The rest, I assume, they got from Jason's laptop. From what the lead detective said, the festival is a go, although the winners may have to wait a bit for their prizes."

They didn't like that, but there wasn't much I could do beyond repeating my statement several more times. A couple of people had some snarky things to say to me, personally.

"Look, I'm just as much a victim as you are," I told one particularly vocal man from the US. He was clad in clothing sporting Confederate flags, and seemed to have an attitude to go with it. "More so because I don't even have my own personal money or credit cards. I don't have a place to stay for the next three days, food, or anything I need, because my luggage was confiscated along with everything else. So yeah, it sucks that my boss is a lying jerkwad, but a little bit of compassion toward those of us who aren't would be greatly appreciated."

"Crazy English bitch," the man said, spitting out a stream of brown tobacco juice perilously near my feet before stomping away in a petulant manner that would have done a cranky toddler proud.

"That's crazy Canadian bitch to you," I called after him, at that moment feeling the weight of the world as several other people closed in around me.

Luckily, the man heading up a traveling circus known as GothFaire, which was hosting the festival, heard the commotion and came over to reassure everyone before anyone else could go for my blood.

"My friends, my very dear friends, do not allow yourself to worry. All is well with the battle of the bands," Dominic, co-owner of the GothFaire, reassured everyone, spreading his hands wide. I was a bit startled to see that he sported fangs, and gave him a good close look, but he didn't appear to have come by them naturally.

That was interesting, I thought to myself as Dominic continued to tell everyone that the Faire would ensure that everyone due a monetary prize would receive it in good order, no matter how the police investigation into Jason's attempted embezzlement was proceeding.

The crowd dispersed at that, all but four young people who looked like they were in their early twenties. They waited until the blond, handsome Dominic moved off to consult with a few of the more vocal bands; then a slight woman with long black hair approached.

"Pardon," she said in a French accent. "What you said, it is true?"

"Yes, absolutely. I don't lie unless it's a life-or-death situation, and even then, I get a bit weird about speaking falsely. I really do have nothing to do with what Jason was pulling—"

"No," she said, glancing back at her companions. "You do not have a place to sleep? We, also, do not. Antoine forgot our tent, and Zuzu was supposed to bring her mother's card, but did not because her mother, she does not approve."

"That's a shame," I said, wondering what they wanted me to do. I had a horrible feeling I was about to be touched, and tightened an arm across my chest, reassured by the slight pressure of my five-hundred-crown bill where I had tucked it into my bra.

"Last night, we found a room. Very quiet, very private, you know? And Antoine, he was looking around, and said there were several other rooms just as quiet. So I thought I would mention that, so that you, too, can sleep."

"I had a room at the hotel—" I started to say, but the young man with hair almost as long and glossy as the woman's moved forward. He looked very much like an Antoine.

"It is not the hotel," he said quickly, then gestured to the southwest, at the edge of the impressive castle that I'd noticed during my march to the festival grounds. "There are stone houses—what is the word? Cabins? And in there, you can sleep out of the weather. They are not warm, but if you have a bedroll, it is cozy."

I let my gaze wander along the west side of the castle, and squinted a little at a couple of pointy stone roofs. "Are those mausoleums? You guys were sleeping in mausoleums? With dead people?"

"Non!" Antoine said, then switched to French. "Two of the cabins are empty inside. There are shelves, yes, where coffins might be placed, but they are empty. The other two are locked. We assumed they were occupied with the ancestors of the castle owner."

I was about to protest that I could do without camping in an empty mausoleum, but the reality was that it was starting to get cold at night, and I could do worse. "Thanks for telling me. I'll see if I can't round up a couple of blankets, and claim the other empty one."

"You must be quick," the fourth member of the band said, a woman with a braided crown of golden hair that was straight out of *Sound of Music*. "The Smashed Avocado has said they want one to sleep in tonight."

"They said they wanted to sleep in the cabin with the bodies," the first woman said, giving a delicate shudder.

"That's horrible," I said, recoiling. "If you know for a fact they are tampering with the remains—"

"No, no," she said, grimacing. "It is not that they want to actually touch the bodies—they simply want to sleep in the crypt with them, you understand? They want to be near them."

"They are very Goth," Antoine said, nodding. "They like that sort of thing."

"Oh. Well …" I tried to decide if it was my problem to warn the GothFaire that one of the bands was likely breaking into an occupied mausoleum if they weren't actually doing harm, but decided that since I didn't know the people in question, I wasn't obligated to alert Dominic and company to what might be going down. "Thanks for the information. And good luck tonight."

They all smiled, wished me well, and hurried off to do whatever groups of young people did before a three-day musical festival. I assumed it involved alcohol, some illegal substances, and probably visits to the services offered by the GothFaire.

"Services," I said thoughtfully, looking to the right, where a U-shaped collection of tents and stands had been arranged. Most of the stands bore signs with graphical depictions of their services and wares, everything from a palm reader, to potions and amulets, a demonologist, a magician, and three different types of diviners—runestone reader, tarot reader, and scryer. "I wonder …"

Ten minutes later, I shook the hand of the fake-fanged Dominic. "You can set up next to the poetry stage," he said, gesturing toward the open side of the U shape.

"I was kind of hoping I could use your tarot reader's booth while she was on bed rest," I told him, not at all impressed by a small stage that was isolated from the bands' main stage. A few beat-up folding chairs had been set out in front of it, while the stage itself, about four square feet, held a wooden three-legged stool, a small battered amp, and a microphone that, like the rest of the equipment, had clearly seen better days.

"It is not possible, *mon ange*," he told me in a French accent that gave me the heebie-jeebies for some reason. He was dressed in what I thought of as classic Vampire Lestat wear, with a black velvet frock coat, gleaming white shirt, elaborate bloodred cravat, and lashings of lace at his wrists. "The tent, it has not even been set up, since the doctor will not allow Reelie to leave her bed until the child is born. You must keep accurate tallies, you understand? Mark down the readings, and then deliver to either Milos or me our share of the money each night."

I wanted to tell him that I was most likely within my rights to set up a tarot-card-reading table outside his Goth-Faire setup and keep all the profits, but decided it wasn't worth the fight. I wasn't happy about handing over half of my take to them, but hopefully, I'd scrape together enough money each day to feed myself and pay for the room reserved at the local hotel. I really did not want to have to sleep in a mausoleum, especially if bands had decided it was cool to break into them and party, as I suspected they were going to do.

"Fine. I should warn you about something that I heard." I told Dominic about the mausoleums, but he didn't seem to be overly worried.

"It is the talk most big, you know?" He gave a shrug that had his shoulder-length blond curls brushing his shoulder. "They do that to scare each other. Ah, there is Milos. I must tell him the latest about Jason Amiri."

"You tried," I told myself, and was about to leave when two big men who looked like they had spent their entire life in a bodybuilding studio, all bulging muscles and tightly fitting sleeveless T-shirts, stopped in front of me at the demonologist's booth.

The men looked like twins since they were bald, had no necks to speak of due to the buildup of shoulder muscles, and both sported identical snake tattoos that coiled around their beefy biceps. I wouldn't have paid any attention except I caught my name.

Not wanting to stare, I turned my back and pulled out my phone, pretending to consult it as I strained my ears.

"I haven't heard of anyone of that name," the demonologist's assistant told them. "Minerva?"

"Goldstein. She is with a thief, the one running the music. He stole something of great importance, and we want it back," one of the big men told her.

"If you see her, you will tell us," the other announced, making it clear there was no option to refuse his request. "We want what the thief stole. You understand?"

"Yes, but I do not know this woman, or the man," the assistant protested.

"You tell us when you see her," the second one repeated. Then they both turned and glanced around the booths, as if figuring out where to go next.

I hurried forward, my mind whirling. Who the hell were those muscle-bound men? And why were they hunting for me? Clearly it was something to do with Jason, but why did I feel like they were talking about something other than the prize pot with which he'd tried to abscond?

My stomach growled as I tried to puzzle it out. After staring hungrily at people clustered around one of the food booths, I decided there were no answers to be found at the fair, and made my sad, lonely, and foodless way to the hotel, where I prayed they wouldn't ask me to verify the credit card information Jason had given to hold my room.

"I'll take a shower, find a cheap meal at a nearby fast-food place, and then go back to the meadow to keep an eye on the bands while avoiding the Muscle Brothers," I told myself as I hurried to the south, where a long hotel sat at the far end of the town. The road, which wound around the meadow up to the castle, was choked with cars and people on foot, the GothFaire having done an excellent job of drawing in seemingly everyone from the Czech Republic to the festivities.

I dodged both people and vehicles, absently pulling out my phone when it burbled a P!nk song at me. "Oh, hell," I said, seeing the name, then with a grimace said, "I hope to god you're not wasting your one phone call on me, Jason, because I am not in a mood to do anything to help you. And speaking of the hellish nightmare you thrust me into, why do you have your phone when the police wouldn't even let me have my money and credit cards, let alone my clothes?"

"Money talks, even in this backwater. As for the rest ... don't start in on me, Minerva," he snapped, his tone far from the urbane one he used when wooing investors. "I've had a day from hell, and I don't need any shit from you. Where are you? Why aren't you here moving your sweet ass to get me out of this nightmare?"

"I like that!" I hurried off into a full parking lot, since a few of the people streaming toward the fair gave me curious looks. "You're the one who tried to run off with the money, leaving me and all the others to deal with your theft."

"I don't need a lecture from you," he said, his voice making me grind my teeth in frustration. "I just need you to do your job and get me out of here. It's dangerous for me to be trapped in a cell. I need to be free. Only free can I be safe."

I rolled my eyes. "Dude, are you off your meds? What are you talking about?"

"I'm telling you," he said, his voice dropping as if someone could overhear him. His voice was a harsh whisper, filled with ire and something that sounded almost like fear. "It's not safe for me here. He's going to come looking for me. Where are you?"

"At the festival. Who is after you? Does this have anything to do with that antique you bought in Paris that you said was going to be worth a fortune?"

"Stop asking stupid questions. I need to see you. Come to the police station. I'll tell the cops to let me see you."

"You're insane, outright insane," I told him. "There's no way in hell I'm going to do any such thing. I have to go now, because *someone* has to deal with the festival that you were supposed to be running."

"Get your ass in here pronto," he demanded. "I need to see you."

I clicked off the call, then, when he called back almost immediately, turned off my phone.

Thankfully, the hotel was of the small mom-and-pop variety, and they'd evidently hadn't heard that Jason was in jail.

"We will let you have your room," a short woman with thick glasses told me as she handed me what looked like an antique metal key. "But you must bring your passport tomorrow. It is the law, you know?"

"I know, and I'll do the best I can to wrestle it away from the police," I promised, praying she wouldn't mention Jason's card that was paying for the room.

That had me thinking as I made my way through a narrow, dark hallway to the ground-floor rooms. What was Jason so afraid of? He'd mentioned in Paris that he'd picked up a valuable item from an antique shop, one that would set him up for life, but he didn't tell me what it was before hustling me off to Prague with the promise of meeting me in Brno.

"It doesn't matter. Jason doesn't matter," I told myself once I got to my tiny room at the back of the hotel. I collapsed down onto the bed, wondering how many nights I'd be able to sleep there if my own cards and money weren't returned. "I just have to get through the next few days; then hopefully the police will return my things."

Brave words for someone whose back is to the wall, my inner narrator said. I sighed at her.

I had a feeling it was going to be a very long night.

THREE

It was the sound that penetrated the depths of water that Ivo imagined embraced him.

He was deep, so very deep in the ocean. Down where the light and sound could not penetrate, just his awareness drifting along without thoughts forming—being, but not alive. Aware, but not thinking. He simply was.

Thump, thump, thump.

He frowned, his consciousness returning from where it had drifted into the depths of his mental ocean, down in the inky abyss from which he wasn't sure he could return.

Thump, thump, thump.

Jangle, jangle.

What was this? His consciousness swam upward, where he knew the light lived. First thumps, and then jangles? Was something happening to his resting spot? No, that could not be. He had been promised sanctuary.

Thump, thump, jangle. Thump. Twang.

No twangs, he said to himself as he continued to move upward through the layers of darkness, his eyes fluttering open. *I draw the line at twangs. The thumping and jangles are enough.*

He broke the surface of the noctambul, shedding the calm that had wrapped around him like a cocoon. And with the shedding came awareness.

First were the sounds, the dull noises now so sharp that they scraped against his ears with the gentleness of a razor blade. The thumping had taken on a rhythmical beat, interspersed with the jangles, and occasional twangs.

Music. Someone was playing music near him. He stared up at the white stone lid of the sarcophagus that was his resting place, but something was wrong. The lid was too far away, and vaulted, like a ceiling.

Voices, sharp and strident, accompanied the noise. He thought for a moment someone was being tortured, but then realized that it was singing. Of a sort. He frowned at the lid that was so wrong, his brain returning to life with a sluggishness that irritated him.

It was at that moment the hunger hit him. He gasped at the pain of it, his body doubling up on itself when he sat up, trying to breathe through the iron grip of pure agony. He half expected to hit his head on the sarcophagus lid, but instead, he found himself staring into the faces of seven people, all frozen in strange postures. Three of the men had instruments strapped to their bodies, while the other four were all women in odd costumes who were standing on the lid of his sarcophagus.

All seven stared at him with identical expressions of sheer, unadulterated horror.

He had a momentary vision of what the situation must look like.

"Boo," he said, unable to keep the word from slipping past his lips.

The screams that followed tore through his head, causing him to clutch at his ears as all seven tried to exit the mausoleum at the same time. There was a jostling of bodies to be the first through the door that would have been comical in any other circumstance, but at that moment, Ivo wanted nothing more than to consume vast quantities of blood, enough to stop the soul-searing agony.

He staggered out after the still-screaming people, his eyes slightly blurry after being unused for so long, but fortunately, night wrapped the world in its indigo embrace, allowing him to force his legs into a lurching gait toward the massive black shape of what had to be Drahanská Castle.

Sounds filled the night air, voices, snatches of soft music, and, in the distance, rustlings of night animals hunting for prey.

Prey. The word echoed in his head, causing him to stumble and clutch at his belly, for a few seconds the pain so great that he couldn't even get air into his lungs.

Light burst out of nowhere, a blue-white light that rose from behind him, casting his shadow against the wall of Drahanská, the figure mangled and twisted as it danced when the light moved behind him. He tried to turn to face whoever had such a powerful lantern, almost falling when he realized the light came from a sleek black automobile, one that seemed to move without sound. He stood staring at it for a few seconds, his mind still slow as the car came to a stop a yard from him. Then suddenly, a shape separated from the auto.

"Ivo? Christ, what are you doing out?"

Ivo squinted at the shape as it moved into the lights cast by the silent auto, his mind grasping for a name. It floated just out of his reach for a few seconds, before it finally allowed itself to be caught. "Finch?"

"You look horrible," Finch said in that straightforward manner that had always amused Ivo. "Why are you here?"

"Thumping," he answered, then because he was an honest man: "Actually, it was the twang that annoyed me the most. There were people. They took my lid off, and were dancing, I think."

"Oh, them," Finch said, with a deep sigh as he cast a glance toward the north side of the castle. "I'll tell Christian they've broken into your mausoleum again. They did it last year, but didn't do anything but leave a bunch of trash behind."

"There's a party going on?" Ivo asked.

"Festival. Come on, since you've emerged from your noctambul, you might as well come in. We have some blood."

Ivo almost moaned at the thought, but something niggled in the back of his mind, a shadow that worried him. He allowed Finch to help him into a side door, slowly and painfully up a staircase, until at last they arrived in what appeared to be a library.

What was it that his mind was hiding from him … ?

"I'll get Christian. He has a special refrigerator with blood, since people tend to end up here needing it. I think it's something to do with the fact that he took over as head of the Moravian Council. Sit down before you fall."

It was something important. Something vital to his well-being.

"Ivo?" Finch's face swam into his view as he swayed slightly. "I would like to ask you if you are all right, but it's clear you're not. Stay here. I'll get Christian and some blood."

Ivo lifted his gaze, seeing not his old friend retreating out of a door, but the memory of a hazy shape that formed into a woman with dark red hair mostly hidden by a large starched white coif. He felt the cool brush of the woman's hand as she dabbed at the blood that seemed to be leaking out of him via a thousand different wounds. He heard the surprise in her voice as she bent over him, saying, "Goodness. A Dark One! You are a surprise."

And then the sensation of life as she pulled up the blue sleeve of her gown, offering him her upper arm, hiding him from the others around them as gratefully he fed. "Go ahead. I've got enough blood to donate to a needy vampire soldier."

Not soldier, he'd wanted to tell her. Doctor. He was a doctor. And she was …

"Beloved," he said on a gasp. The world spun, filled with black blotches, and he fell back into the dark abyss that had held him for so long.

Once again, it was sound that pulled his awareness from the depths of insensibility.

"—don't see why he can't simply drink it if it's helping, which it clearly is."

"It's helping because he has been in a state of noctambul, and thus, his body is deprived to the point where any blood that can be ingested will be tolerated. For a while. Once he is back to full health, however, he will likely begin to decline again. Thus it is for those whose Beloveds are taken from them."

Ivo gave a mental frown at the man speaking, forcing his mind to the surface again so he could speak. "She wasn't taken from me," he managed to say, his eyes refusing to co-operate and open. "I didn't even see her clearly, let alone have a connection of any sort."

"Ah, you are awake again. Good."

That had to be Christian Dante, Finch's uncle. Ivo had a vague memory of him, a man with dark hair and incredibly bright silver eyes. With an effort, he pulled one hand up to his face, removing the cloth that covered his eyes. Instantly, light penetrated his brain, causing him to wince and squint. "Ow. Where are we, the surface of the sun?"

Two figures swam into view and, after a couple of seconds, resolved themselves into Finch and his uncle. "Not quite," Finch answered, giving him a disgruntled look. Finch frequently looked disgruntled, Ivo mused to himself as stud-ied first his old friend, then the man who had helped save him from certain death. "But it is a bit hellish outside what with all the mortals carrying on."

Christian Dante made a face. "I've secured your parents' mausoleum, but it makes no sense to worry about protecting the empty ones until after the festival is over. Ivo can stay here with us until that time."

"You keep mentioning a festival," Ivo said, running a hand over his jaw. "Why on earth are you holding one here?"

"It's a tradition started twenty or so years ago. How do you feel?" Christian asked.

Ivo took inventory of his limbs. "I have a dull headache in the front of my head, but everything else seems to be functioning. Did I hear you say I fed? From whom?"

"What, not whom," Finch answered, pulling a container

from a small wicker basket. "I'm not personally acquainted with the pigs who donated their blood, but it evidently agreed with you."

"It won't for long," Christian warned, giving Ivo a long, steady look that made him uncomfortable, just as if his soul had been laid bare for the older man.

The headache pulsed as he sagged back against pillows that had been arranged to prop him up on a bed. "So I'm back to where I was before?"

"If by that, you mean did we find your Beloved, no," Finch said, exchanging glances with his uncle. "We tried for years, Ivo. It was difficult during the war, but once it ended—"

"It did end? I'm glad to hear that. How?"

"Germany signed an armistice two years after you were injured," Finch said, his expression solemn now. "I'll bring you a tablet so you can read about what you missed. Assuming you'd like to do that."

The dull ache that he had been aware of gripped him, driving home the utter uselessness of existence. "A tablet of what? No, it doesn't matter. I don't want to know. I don't want to be if you didn't find the woman who ruined my life. I just want to go back underwater and drift."

"Underwater?" Finch asked, then shook his head. "We did search for her, Ivo. For years. We damned near examined every woman in that region of France, not to mention the bulk of nurses. A few died. If your Beloved was one of them …"The sentence finished awkwardly.

Ivo nodded, his soul as depressed as the rest of him. "Then there's no hope. I know. I've known since you dragged my carcass here … what year is it?"

"Two thousand two."

He blinked a couple of times at that, but resumed his sentence. "Since you dragged me here eighty-six years ago. You don't have to look so guilty, Finch. I know that you and Christian have done all you can. It is what it is. I am resigned to that. I just want to go back to my watery not-grave."

Finch frowned, and asked his uncle, "Has water seeped into the mausoleum?"

"I believe Ivo is speaking metaphorically." Christian gave him another piercing look. "Naturally, you are welcome to resume a state of noctambul, but I would advise you to wait a few days after the end of the festival More blood is available for as long as your body is willing to tolerate it. Judging by the past, I assume that to be a week or possibly two."

"The mortals are annoying, but they make for an interesting study," Finch said, rubbing his chin.

Ivo plucked at the down comforter covering him. "Don't tell me you're writing another book on how to live an organized life?"

"Er ... not another," Finch admitted, clearing his throat. "It's the same one, actually. I'm just putting some finishing touches to it now."

Ivo cocked an eyebrow.

"Yes, yes, I know, you've written copious volumes of poetry while I'm still working on one book, but with all due respect, your poetry can't be compared to the work demanded by my book. Making organization out of chaos isn't easy, you know."

"I said nothing," Ivo said, smiling to himself. He hadn't thought of his poetic phase in a very long time. There was a point where he'd been convinced that he was destined to be a poet of Byron's level, but the public's reception to his slim volumes of poetry had been disappointing in the extreme. The few reviews he'd garnered didn't offer him much solace. Especially the one that referred to him as writing "sophomoric, somnambulistic drivel that couldn't keep a terrier awake in a room filled with rats."

"You didn't have to. I can feel you thinking it," Finch responded, looking irritated. He gave a little sniff, and added, "Regardless, you might as well stay awake until the mortals have finished their celebration."

"You might actually enjoy seeing them," Christian told him, moving toward the door. "They can be vastly entertaining, and it will do much to bring you up to date by studying them."

"A festival?" Ivo scratched at a spot on the side of his head, feeling dusty and itchy. He would bathe, he decided. That and some fresh garments, which no doubt Finch would lend him, would make him feel better. If he had to stay awake for a few more days, then he might as well be comfortable, even if he was in mental, emotional, and physical hell. "What sort of festival?"

"Music, for the most part, which can either be very good or atrociously bad. A traveling fair hosts it, which is entertaining in itself. Go out and see how the mortals have changed since you went noctambul. Then, when they have left, we'll get you settled again," Christian told him, and with a nod at Finch left the room.

"Your family," Ivo said with a little shake of his head.

Finch looked somewhat martyred. "I know. You don't need to say it. They've always had a weakness for mortals. They're always trying to protect them, even when it's against their interests."

"You're the one who became a doctor," Ivo pointed out, smiling just a little at the memory of their time training in Germany. "Even your father didn't do that."

"No, he was too busy being James Bond," Finch said with a grimace.

"Who?"

"A literary character. I'll find some of the books for you. You might like them. They're dated, but some of the movies are well done."

"Ah, the cinema. I always enjoyed that." Ivo felt a little spike of interest. Perhaps remaining on the surface for a few days would be a good idea. If nothing else, it would give him something new to think about for his submersion.

The next five hours were eye-opening, to say the least. Finch introduced him to a number of modern devices that seemed to make life incredibly easy, everything from the tablet he kept mentioning—and which turned out to be a miraculous device that Ivo half suspected was magic in origin—to thick rectangles that Finch claimed were personal traveling telephones.

By the time morning's light had stretched across the sky, Ivo felt sufficiently in touch with modernity that he was confident he could pass without risk of undue attention amongst the mortals who congregated outside Christian's castle.

"Get some rest," Finch said as the two men clung to the shadows as they returned from a stable that had been converted into a garage. "We can go out this evening, once the sun has set. Are you hungry?"

"Yes," Ivo answered. "But not desperately so. I will not partake of the pig's blood, if that's what you were going to offer next. Rest does sound good, however. My muscles feel as if they have been stretched too tight."

Finch eyed him as they entered the castle. "You look better, but you're too thin. You should feed as much as possible before you go noctambul again."

"Possibly," Ivo said, holding tight to the magic tablet that Finch told him he could use to catch up. He particularly was looking forward to some quiet time so he could investigate something called AOL. During the brief tour of it that Finch had conducted, Ivo had noticed a video of a cat doing a belly dance, and he very much wanted to see that. "I'll see you later, then?"

"Yes. I need to work more on my book, but let me know when you're ready to go to the festival, and I'll put it aside."

They parted, and after an extremely entertaining two hours wherein Ivo found a plethora of dancing-cat videos, which then led to dogs playing in snow, and somehow to a woman in the States with plentiful tattoos who was filmed shearing placid, round sheep, he fell asleep with the tablet clutched to his chest.

Several hours later, the music drew him from the castle. He didn't want to disturb Finch if he was working on his book, and since Christian was nowhere to be found, Ivo strolled down to the meadow where a big wooden stage had been set up, black metal scaffolding surrounding both sides and the back of it, while in front, a sea of blankets and small chairs rippled back toward the road that led up to Drahanská.

Snatches of conversation in a variety of languages—mostly Czech, but some German, French, and English—wove a tapestry around him as he strolled toward bright lights that had been set up to the east.

"—not as good as the Pillowed Pigeon Eaters, but what do you expect from ska?"

"Dude! Did you see that Goth chick? Her nips were double pierced. Double pierced!"

"—and I'm not in the mood for this attitude, Jakob. Open means open for both of us, not just you. If you don't like me banging other men, then maybe you need to keep your dick in your pants, and not be constantly sticking it in every hole you can find."

The crowd, which had been streaming away from the stage, were all headed in the same direction. Ivo followed with them, pausing at the end of what must be the traveling fair that Christian had mentioned.

A small wooden platform sat to his left with a couple of metal chairs scattered in front of it. Clearly it was a stage of some sort. Just beyond it, a man sat hunched in a chair, a packing box between him and a woman with the most glorious red hair he'd ever seen. No, not red, he corrected himself, copper. A bright, glossy copper that, even in the blue-white lights that hung illuminating the fair, glowed with life. The woman appeared to be playing a card game.

Ivo was no stranger to card games, having played them with mortals while he served in the British medical corps. Despite his best attempts, he was never able to keep from being fleeced by the company sharps, and he cast a suspicious look now toward the woman. No doubt she was taking the poor, unsuspecting man for all of his funds. The foolish mortal wasn't even watching the cards; he was staring at her with a lascivious look that for some reason Ivo found offensive. He took a step toward the stage, intent on discovering if she was a card sharp and was purposely beguiling the man with her glorious hair, but before he could do so, he was accosted by a small woman with bleached white hair that stuck up like a hedgehog's.

"Are you here for the poetry slam?" she asked him.

"No, I—slam?"

"Yes." She nodded toward the small stage, and consulted a clipboard, on which was a sheet of lined paper. It was empty of all writing. "Luckily, I can just fit you into the schedule. Name?"

"Ivo Zeman," he told her, about to protest that he didn't want to slam anything, let alone poetry, of which he had a fondness despite society's refusal to view him as the twentieth century's version of Lord Byron.

"Excellent. You may take the stage," the woman said, then snatched up an oblong black device, flipped a switch on it, and spoke into it, saying, "Welcome to tonight's poetry slam. Up first, we have Ivo Zeman, from … ?" She looked at him.

"Bucharest," he answered.

"From Romania. Take it away, Ivo!"

She handed him the device, then backed up a few steps, applauding lightly.

A few people who drifted past the area cast him a curious glance, but no one sat down to watch him slam.

Ivo pursed his lips, slid a glance toward the shining-hair woman who was still in the middle of demonstrating some card trick to her mark, and decided there was no better place to keep an eye on her than the stage. He stepped onto it, holding the device up to his mouth, startled when his voice blasted out of a small red-and-black box behind him. "Good evening. Er …"

"Hold it a few inches from your mouth," the clipboard woman said before she hurried off.

"Very well. Poetry." He spoke to the people who headed

toward the main part of the fair, dredging through his memory for his most effective poem. "It is a subject near and dear to my heart. I will now recite for you the opening stanzas of my opus." He cleared his throat, sliding a glance toward the woman. She was alone now, her mark having no doubt given her all he had, leaving her to shuffle her cards with dexterity that bespoke familiarity. She was also not paying him one whit of attention.

O tender night, circling sweetly in the sky,
Now a cloud, now a drape across my desperate view.
O pure lily, soft and cool, dim Death to me,
Delicate shroud binding, hiding, blinding.
Your stretching fingers drag me down to the depths of hell
Evergreen in ever-dying coals of despair.
Aloft in the night, smothering my thoughts and dreams
Until at my last hope shrivels and drops to the earth.
Futility has claimed me for another day.

He bowed his head at the last word, feeling that he had never performed as well as that moment.

"Dude," came a voice next to him.

He slid a glance over to the source. The shining-hair woman was staring at him with an expression of what he could only assume was profound appreciation.

"Madam," he said, giving her a little bow of acknowledgment.

"Duuude," she said again, this time drawing out the word.

"You might be interested to know that that was the opening stanza to 'Ever-Present Blight upon the Seared Remains of My Soul,' my most profound work."

"Yeah, it's something all right." She shook her head, the curtain of hair shimmering around her, making him think of streams of molten copper. "Was it supposed to rhyme? I don't know a lot about poetry, but the ones I remember from when I was a child all rhymed."

"Madam," he repeated, this time in as haughty a tone as he could summon. He looked down his nose at her, sensing criticism hovered behind her inquiry. "Blank verse does not rhyme."

"Is that what it is?" Her face scrunched up in a manner that he should have found disfiguring but, to his annoyance, just rendered her freckled countenance adorably delightful. "I mean, I've heard about emo poetry, but that—boy, that really is something unique, huh? It's very Victorian, too. Did you mean for it to sound that way?"

Ivo wasn't entirely certain that she was criticizing the best of all his poems. Could it be that he was so out of touch with modern mortals that what he thought at first might be a negative reaction was, in fact, high praise? "The poem may seem a bit dated, but I stand behind it," he said after a moment's consideration of how best to deal with her question. "Are you fond of poetry?"

"Not really," she said, giving him a little smile that he felt down to the tips of his toenails. "But that's probably because I haven't ever tried reading it. I'm very big on novels, though. Especially historical romances. All those lords and ladies doing the Jane Austen thing. So fun."

He stared at her, trying to pick through her sentence, feeling oddly as if he were floating in an ocean, and waves kept drawing him under the surface, only for him to pop up and gasp for air. "Historical romances?" he asked, searching his memory again. "Jane Austen, yes, I am aware of her. I seem to also recall being entertained by Maria Edgeworth and Ann Radcliffe."

"Those are a bit older than the types I normally read," she said slowly, giving him an odd look. "Do you—this is going to sound rude, but I could swear I know you. Were you at the festival yesterday?"

"No." He stepped off the stage, moving over to where she sat, noting that a sign had been written and propped up on her far side, informing him that she read tarot cards. "Those are tarot cards you have? I thought you were performing acts of card sharkery."

"I'm not absolutely certain that sharkery is an actual

word, but yes, they are tarot cards. I'm a cartomancer. Would you like a reading?"

He consulted the sign, thinking of the five thousand Czech crowns that Finch had given him, telling him he might want to buy something at the fair. He sat down, carefully placing the tablet on the crate while keeping one hand resting on it, since it was his most precious possession. "Three hundred crowns is agreeable. You may proceed with the reading."

She eyed the tablet. "You might want to move your … er … what is that?"

"Windows XP Tablet," he said, allowing a note of pride to creep into his voice. "My friend Finch has loaned it to me. He purchased it in the States from a man named Gates, and brought it home. No one in Moravia has one like it."

"Huh. Tablet. Is it like a big mobile phone?"

"Yes?" Ivo answered, hoping that was true.

"Gotcha. Well, if you will move your fancy big-ass Microsoft mobile phone, I'll do a spread for you."

He was mildly shocked until he realized that it was the cards she would be spreading.

"So, what I generally do is shuffle the cards a few times, then cut them until you're happy with them. If you want, you can cut them yourself. I don't mind if others touch my cards. Some readers do, but eh. They're bits of paper and ink, you know? And the lamination has peeled off of some of them, so they're glued back together, but it's what they say that matters, not what they are, if you get me."

Ivo listened to her with part of his attention, the rest of his mind wondering at the fact that he found her so enticing beyond her hair. He studied her as she shuffled the cards, noting a heart-shaped face that was heavily freckled, a frame that was in no way delicate, but pleasing in its curves, and breasts that he could not help but approve of. He wondered about her hips, ass, and legs, but he was a gentleman, and gentlemen did not ogle those who were reading their fortunes.

No matter how tempting they were.

"You want to cut, or should I?" she asked, holding the deck of well-used cards.

"I'll do it," he said, a tiny voice in his head warning that she might well be sharking him. He took the cards, the brush of her fingers against his hand sending a streak of heat so great that he jerked his hand back.

"Ow," she said, laughing and shaking her hand. "That was a hell of a static shock, huh? Go ahead and cut them as many times as you like."

He laid four piles of cards in front of them, then gathered them back in a random order before setting the stack on the table.

"I can do a simple three-card spread, or a more detailed five-card that goes into specific concerns you might have. Which would you prefer?" she asked, her hand poised over the cards.

"Five cards," he said, picking it simply because he assumed it would keep her speaking the longest. He liked her voice. It was lilting despite the American accent. They spoke in English, but she definitely had a way of pronouncing some words that had him wondering if she'd spent time in Ireland.

"Here we go, then. First card, four of cups. This stands for your past, and it represents a withdrawal, or refusal. It says you may be overthinking something, that you might be stuck on a choice, and are spinning your wheels."

"Spinning my wheels," he repeated, thinking of his visit to Christian's garage. "My friend's uncle has a motorcycle. I liked it the best of all his vehicles. I rode a Triumph motorcycle when I was in France, and enjoyed it greatly. My friend said I could try his uncle's motorcycle, although I understand it is much more powerful."

"I'm not much for anything beyond a Vespa, but you do you," she told him.

He realized then that he had not inquired as to her name. "I am Ivo."

"Yeah, I heard the woman say your name."

She laid another card down in front of him. "The Emperor."

"What is your name?" he asked, since she didn't seem to take the hint.

"Minerva Goldstein. The Emperor in the present spot is more or less a sign that your mind needs structure. It says that you might be feeling powerless, and you will continue to do so until you stand your ground, and reclaim your authority."

"Do you know Finch?" he asked, suspicious.

"The little birds? Sure. They're cute."

"Finch is a person. My friend." Ivo thought for a few seconds. "My closest friend."

"Ah, your partner?" The look she flickered his way seemed to be somewhat disappointed. "I'm afraid I don't know anyone with that name."

"I thought you might. He is a strong believer in an ordered mind. He's writing a book about that."

"Good for him. Right, the card in your future spot is three of swords. Ouch. This is kind of a mental-housecleaning card, but it can also mean that your heart has been attacked, but you are still strong, and you can heal and move past that stage. I like to think of it as a card that says that the skies are clearing, and the worst is over."

"That would be nice if it was so, but I doubt if it can be true. Not unless you happen to know of a woman around a hundred years old who used to live in France," he answered, his heart glum.

She shot him an odd look, but placed down another card. "This is the first of two cards that explain what the universe is trying to tell you. It can be a warning, a hint, or even a commentary of something going on in your life. Your card is the queen of swords. That says to me that you are pretty strong-willed and don't tolerate fools gladly, but you may be allowing yourself to be influenced by the past. You won't be happy until you can let that go."

"You seem to be focused on events in my past," Ivo said, wondering if she wasn't pulling some sort of con after all.

It seemed unlikely, but the memories of the soldiers in the trenches were all too strong. "Is there a reason for that?"

She frowned at the cards for a moment before her gaze met his. He noticed that what he'd first thought were dark brown eyes were actually blue, a midnight blue with little flecks that seemed to glitter in the artificial light. "That's odd. I didn't realize I was doing that, but you're right. It's as if the cards are focused on your past, and not anything else. Odd. Well, let's go on to the last card. This is a second sign from the universe, more something to think about than an action that's being demanded of you. Oh."

Ivo looked with interest at the card. It was a woman holding an odd-shaped goblet, with several others below her, and a figure in a cloak moving away in the distance. "Is it bad?"

"No, eight of cups isn't a bad card at all." She bit her lip for a second, then looked up at him again. "It's a journey card. It says that you are on the path of a journey into the unknown."

"At last, a card that doesn't harp on my past," he said, nodding with approval even though the only journey he would be taking was back to his mausoleum.

"Actually …" She gave a wry smile. "I'm afraid it does deal with your past. Because this journey that you're about to start can only happen if you release the fears of your past. In effect, you're walking away from something that no longer works for you. Does that make any sense?"

"No," he said, and pulled money out of his pocket, placing it before her.

"Are you sure?" Minerva looked puzzled, her eyes scanning the cards. "My readings are usually dead-on. Maybe you're just not admitting something to yourself—"

"I have no future, so your cards are faulty," he said firmly, standing, but strangely loath to leave her. She might be all wrong with her tarot reading, but that didn't mean he wanted to part company. Far from it. "Have you seen the fair? I have not, but it looks interesting. Perhaps you would like to accompany me?"

"Actually—" she started to say, but stopped, her eyes growing round when two men pushed themselves around Ivo.

"You. We haven't talked to you. We are looking for a woman named Minerva Goldstein. You know her?" one of the two said, leaning over Minerva, his fists on her makeshift table.

Her expression was frozen, but Ivo saw a flash of fear in her eyes that instantly had him moving around to her side so that he could face the two men. They were large, like circus strongmen, but Ivo didn't like the air of menace that rolled off them.

"Who ... uh ..." Minerva swallowed, clearly unwilling to identify herself to the men, and Ivo didn't blame her.

"Who are you asking about?" Ivo asked, draping his arm casually across Minerva's shoulders. They twitched at the contact, but to his surprise—and a brief spurt of pleasure— she leaned into him.

One of the men repeated the name. "She is with a thief. He stole a spell, a valuable spell," the second added, his eyes narrowed on Ivo. "You know her?"

"No," he said, meeting the gaze without so much as a flicker of an eyelash. "And neither does my ... my fiancée. Isn't that right, Persephone?"

Minerva's lips parted as she slanted a look up at him, blinking twice before she managed to say, "That's right, Ivo. You said someone stole a spell? Like ... a *spell* spell?"

"A spell, yes. The kind you cast," the first man said, his lip curling up. He pointed at Ivo. "You are mundane? Ask the Dark One. He will explain about spells."

Minerva seemed to turn to stone beside him. Ivo gave a mental sigh. He didn't mind people knowing what he was, but if she was a mortal being, then he'd be obligated to explain to her what Dark Ones were, and she'd no doubt be terrified of him. Everyone feared Dark Ones. "What does this spell do?" he asked, hoping to distract Minerva from his origins.

The second strongman frowned at him. "It's valuable, OK? That's all you need to know. If you see this Minerva Goldstein, then tell us. We'll take care of the rest."

"Why …" Minerva gave a little cough. "Why do you want her? You said someone else stole the spell."

"She knows where her partner hid it," the first man said, straightening up before turning to the other one. "Maybe she's with the music people. We'll go check there."

"There's so many of them," the second complained. "And I'm hungry."

"You just ate," the first said sternly as they retreated. Ivo took a few steps after them, torn between accosting them, and allowing them to leave, since they clearly distressed Minerva.

"How do you expect me to intimidate everyone unless I keep my strength up? Besides, you ate six hamburgers, and I only had five."

"You had two sausages with your burgers," the first argued as they moved into the crowd. "That counts for one burger."

Ivo watched them a few more seconds, then turned to ask Minerva what that was all about.

She was gone. The handwritten sign announcing her tarot card reading fluttered in the cool night air next to her empty chair, and the equally empty makeshift table.

No, not empty. He moved over to catch a scrap of blue paper as the wind lifted it.

Hotel was written on the paper. *Room evergreen in ever-dying coals of despair.*

Ivo pursed his lips, wondering exactly what the cryptic note meant. Was she mocking him? Or was this a way of alerting him to something … like her hotel room number?

And if it was the latter, why did he so badly want to see her again when he had no future with her?

No future at all.

FOUR

"Omigod, omigod, omigod." I scurried behind a line of trucks and vans that were used to carry the equipment for the stage, my heart beating so loudly I could feel it throb in my ears. I paused at the end of one of the big trucks and glanced around, but there was no one nearby, so with a muttered oath at the light rain that had hit the area that morning, I crawled under the truck and tried to hide myself behind one of its big tires.

To: Jason Amiri

What the hell? What the ever-living hell, Jason? You stole a spell? While we were in Paris, you stole a spell? Was it when you were in that antique shop? It was, wasn't it? Dammit! It's not bad enough you tried to embezzle the festival funds, you also stole a spell? Two massive thief takers are after me because of you. And when I say massive, I mean muscles upon muscles upon muscles sort of massive. The massive that can break you without even trying. WHY DID YOU STEAL A SPELL AND TELL PEOPLE I KNOW WHERE IT IS?

Fortunately for my mental state, it wasn't long before Jason replied to my text.

From: Jason Amiri

For fuck's sake, why do you think I told you to come here? We could have straightened this all out if you'd just done what I'd told you to do, but no. You had to be a bitch about it all.

To: Jason Amiri

You, sir, are an asshat.

To: Jason Amiri

The hattiest of all asses.

To: Jason Amiri

And for the record, I am not now, nor am I ever, going to see you again.

To: Jason Amiri

Unless it's in court, and you're being charged. Then I'll happily testify like the wind against you.

From: Jason Amiri

Stop texting me! The guard told me I could keep my phone if I didn't use it to contact anyone. I can only delete your messages so fast. They'll catch me if you keep at it. I'm turning off my phone now. Don't bother me again unless it's to tell me when you're coming in to see me. Otherwise, have fun with the thief takers, ha ha ha.

"Asshat," I said aloud, grinding my teeth a little at the man for whom I'd worked only a week. "Seven days too long."

I lay on the cold, damp ground for a few minutes more, listening for sounds of the burly twins, but heard no one speaking in their deep tones. By the time I emerged from my hiding place, I was cold, my entire front side was damp and muddy, and I was hungry again because the Scary Twins just had to mention burgers and sausages.

"I have to distract myself," I said softly as I glanced toward the big stage. The next band due to perform was already in place, doing a brief sound check as people started filling the area in front of them. Guilt drove me to a spot behind the stage, where a woman with bloodred hair was ordering everyone around. "I'm just checking in to make sure everything is running all right," I said when she spun around to glare at me.

"Oh, it's you. Has your partner returned the money you stole?" she asked with a toss of her head. "Dominic and Milos are not happy!"

"I didn't steal anything, and the police have the money, yes, which in fact Dominic knows because I told him so myself."

"*Tch,*" the woman—whose name I thought was Tanya—said with another dramatic flare of her nostrils. "Police will never give up money. It is their way."

"I just figured I'd make sure everything was running smoothly," I said a bit lamely, not wanting to stay around the area if the thief takers were going to be nosing around. I hadn't introduced myself to too many people—most of them simply thought I was Jason's secretary—but I didn't want to take any chances. Not where thief takers were concerned.

What spell had Jason stolen? It had to be worth a whole lot of money if the Big Twins had been sent after him.

"It is organized, yes, although I am not doing this again," Tanya answered, biting off each word. "Next year, someone else will handle the festival. No, you are not on now. I have told you five times already! You go on after the Germans!"

I backed away as she rounded on a group of tall, skinny young men all dressed in black. It appeared to me that Tanya had everything well in hand, so I could leave the festival with a clear conscience.

And go back to my hotel room.

Did Ivo find my note? Would he show up? Was there a reason I had sensed his past was so important to his present? And why did I keep remembering a time in my distant past, when I'd stumbled across a vampire that was almost dead? I tried to remember what the man had looked like, but he was so wounded, I had little impression other than that of an impossible amount of blood. No mortal being could have survived it.

And so I'd fed him, hoping that my donation of blood might help him get over the worst of his injuries.

"It can't be him," I told myself as I skirted the edge of the festival grounds, glancing up at the castle that loomed overhead, its tall towers aglow with warm, golden pools of light, the upper ramparts melting seamlessly into the darkness of the night sky. "That's too much of a coincidence. Isn't it?"

On the long walk back to my hotel, I pondered this and the question of why I had given Ivo an invitation to visit me. There was something about him, an intangible need that thrummed within him, almost immediately finding an answer in me that had led me to scribble out a line of his atrocious poetry.

"It's called human kindness," I told myself a half hour later, when I arrived at the hotel, avoiding the eyes of the night clerk as I slipped into my ground-floor room, giving the room number—six—a little nod. "Anything higher than room eight, and I would have been in trouble. Although I'm not sure if I could have stood more lines of his emo poetry. Eight was plenty."

I wished I had something else to change into other than the dress I'd worn flying out from Prague, but there was little I could do about that. Instead of fretting, I pulled out my cards.

I shuffled the cards slowly, my fingers idly feeling all the bumps, tears, and thickened spots where I'd glued them back together, all the while wondering if I should ask the cards a specific question. "Would you tell me what I want to know this time?" I asked them as I spread them out facedown in a fan. "Or would you pull your usual shenanigans and answer something that I didn't ask you?"

My fingers drifted across the cards as I let my inner senses come to the fore, causing my hands to tingle as they passed over certain cards, which I flipped over until four lay before me.

I sighed, and tapped the cards one after the other as I summed them up. "Romance. Happiness in relationships. Love, commitment, and undying devotion. And peril. Great. I'm going to fall in love with someone, and face a dire situation because of it. Sounds like an abusive relationship to me. No, thank you, cards. I'd rather stay single forever than put up with that sort of crap."

I gathered up the cards, shuffled them automatically, and glanced out the window, wondering if Ivo was going to stop by, or if he would wait until the following day.

"He's a vampire. He doesn't go out during the day; thus, he's not going to be here until tomorrow night, if he bothers to see you at all," I told myself after another half hour. I peeled off my dress, washed my underwear and bra, set them to dry on the radiator, and donned one of the festival T-shirts given to all the band members. I'd blatantly stolen the largest one I could find from the stack that the testy Tanya had handed out to the bands the day before, but I decided a little theft was allowed considering I needed something to sleep in.

I was just sitting on the bed, feeling very lonely, and on the verge of a bona fide pity party. "Why don't I have someone?" I asked the top of my head, which was all I could see in the mirror above a small sink. "I'm a hundred and eighteen years old. Surely I should have someone in my life by now?"

My inner voice *tsk*ed at me. "Let's not go down the maudlin path," I told the *tsk*er. "I look like a normal woman in her late thirties—not pretty, but not hideous. I'm not a horrible person. I deserve someone nice. Someone interesting. Someone ..." My mind faltered, unable to bring forward the words I wanted. I wasn't even sure what they were, since I never had been able to describe a man who fit my idea as a perfect mate.

"Fine. Pity party it is," I said on a sigh, shaking the duvet.

A knock sounded before I had one leg inserted beneath it.

My breath stopped in my throat for a second while I stared at the door. Then suddenly, I was there, opening it, happiness filling me at the thought that Ivo had decided to visit me after all. I spoke even before I had the door fully open. "I'm so glad you—holy shitsnacks!"

The man who stood there was, indeed, Ivo, but it was an Ivo who looked like he'd been pulled through a hedge backward. Twice. After which, he was run over by a lawn mower.

"Good evening, Minerva," he said, making a little bow that turned into a wince halfway down. He held a ragged bouquet of flowers that was mostly leaves and stems to which a few chrysanthemum flower heads clung drunkenly. He thrust them at me. "I brought you flowers as a token of my esteem. I have also composed a few lines in your honor."

"What the hell happened to you?" I asked, my gaze moving from his face—one side of which was streaked black with what appeared to be dirt, oil, and blood—on down to his shirt. His left sleeve was torn off, exposing the side of his forearm that oozed fresh blood, also speckled with dirt. His shirt had an artistic spray of blood across that side, and the left leg of his pants appeared to have been hacked off just below the knee with a dull instrument. His left shoe was missing completely. "Are you OK?"

"I'm fine," he said, entering the room when I backed up to let him in, my gaze moving from one injury to the next as I tried to understand what on earth could have happened in the space of an hour. He waggled a hand in a gesture of nonchalance.

His pinkie fingernail fell off.

"There was a slight contretemps with Christian's motorcycle," he said, trying to scoot the fingernail aside with the foot still clad in a shoe. "It does not run in the same manner as the ones I am familiar with."

"Contretemps … dude! It looks like the motorcycle ran over you a few times."

"Well …" He started to make another gesture, glanced at his hand, and stopped. "It did once or twice, but only because I was unfamiliar with its workings. And then my trousers were caught on some protuberance that emerged from the wheels, but later, after I extricated my left shoe from where it had become stuck, all ran well. For the most part. Until I hit a few patches of gravel. The gravel in this area is much different than French gravel I have traveled on."

I stared at him for a few seconds, unsure if I should burst into laughter, or take care of his obvious wounds.

Years of medical training won out. "Sit down," I told him, moving to the sparse bathroom to wet a towel and grab the bar of soap I'd used earlier to wash my clothes.

"I would like to recite the few lines I have dedicated in your honor," he told me, frowning when I emerged from the bathroom. "And I cannot do so sitting. What do you think you are going to do with that?"

"Tend your wounds. Sit."

He frowned at the soap.

"Please," I added.

He sighed, and did as I requested. "Very well, but I can assure you that I have no need of medical care. I am fully qualified as a physician."

"So am I," I told him, and started at his face, carefully cleaning the road rash grime off his cheek.

"You are?" He looked surprised, then flinched when I hit a particularly gruesome bit on his cheekbone. "I have heard that some women sought degrees in medical care, but all the women I knew were nurses."

"Yes, well, that sort of thinking went out a century ago," I told him, rinsing out the washcloth, and returning to clean up his arm. "As a matter of fact, I started out as a nurse, but by the time World War Two hit, I managed to get fully trained as a doctor. Not that anyone would let me practice, but at least I made my point."

"You treat mortals, then?" he asked.

"Not now. It's difficult to keep getting licensed when you're not mortal. Usually, I take a decade off when I get to the point where people start wondering why I'm not aging, then decide if I want to go through medical school again under a new identity to get recertified. Not that the mortals know it's recertification, but eh. That's why I'm working as a translator now. It's easier, documentation-wise. Ouch. I can't do anything about your missing fingernail, but that cut along the side of your hand looks deep. Hang on. There's a hand towel I can tear up and use as a bandage."

"I have no need for a bandage," he called after me as I

went to the bathroom again, cleaning the washcloth. "I am a Dark One. I will heal with time. It's just that I'm a little …"

"A little what?" I asked when I had bandaged up his left hand. He sat on the bed looking oddly deflated, his gaze on the floor as if his thoughts were turned inward. I touched his bare shoulder. "Ivo?"

"Hmm?" He looked up.

"Nothing. Why don't you put your foot on the bed so I can wipe the blood and dirt off your ankle."

"There is no need—" he started to protest.

"I know, but this way, you won't spread blood everywhere."

He made a little face of disagreement but, after kicking off his remaining shoe, swung both legs on the bed, lying back. I wiped off his gory ankle, noting that the blood was already slowing and thickening, indicating that his natural healing abilities were kicking in.

"Why did those two strongmen think that you had a stolen spell?" he asked, his uninjured arm behind his head as he looked at the ceiling.

"No clue. My boss is currently enjoying the hospitality of the local police because he tried to skip out with the money from the music festival, but I had no idea he also stole something valuable like a spell. To be honest, I didn't know you could steal a spell." I finished with his leg and, noting that a little fresh blood had oozed out of the carnage on his cheek, twisted the washcloth to a clean section, and leaned over him, intending on dabbing at it.

Memory swamped me, along with a strong sense of need, a pulsing red hunger that roared to life with a ferocity that left me shaking. I gasped, staring down at Ivo as he stared back at me, his eyes wide, his pupils flaring.

"It *is* you," I said, goose bumps rippling down from my head to my extremities. "I wondered, but I wasn't sure. …"

He stared at me as if he were seeing a ghost; then suddenly, I was lying across him, his mouth hot on mine.

"Wow, you're … hoo! You didn't let that motorcycle falling on you damage any of these muscles … whoa, dude!

I am going commando! You can't put your hand there!" I squirmed when one of Ivo's hands went wandering down my back to where my butt was barely covered by the oversized tee. I stared down at him, my mouth feeling simultaneously sensitized, and thrilled with the situation.

"How can this be?" Ivo managed to say, his eyes crossing when I couldn't resist the lure of his lips again, taking care not to put any pressure on his scraped cheek as I kissed him. He waited until I stopped sucking his tongue before adding, "You're dead."

"I assure you that I am very much not dead," I said, reaching behind me to stop the hand that had retreated but was once again sliding toward my ass. "Oh, no you don't. I'm not saying that I won't let you later on, because you really got my motor humming with that kiss, but I have at least a dozen questions that I'd like answered, first."

"You are my Beloved," he said, looking first stunned, then mildly indignant. "If you are not dead and some form of corporeal spirit, then you are alive."

"No one can say that you lack the ability to grasp the basics of a situation," I answered, wanting to giggle at him, but feeling that somehow, I'd just dealt him a blow, and a little kindness was better suited to the situation. "But yes, I am alive."

His brows pulled together, his hands moving off me. I felt the withdrawal of him as if he'd turned to ice. "Then you deliberately hid yourself from me. You wished for my existence to be a torment. You tricked Finch and Christian in an attempt to drive me to noctambul."

Carefully, so as not to hurt anything on his torso that might have been bruised in what was obviously a hairy ride to the hotel, I eased off him, and sat on my heels close enough to touch him, but feeling oddly isolated. "I didn't hide from anyone, let alone trick people into tormenting you. Ivo, I feel like we're talking at cross-purposes. It was you I saw in 1916 in France, yes? You were gravely injured? Like almost blown-apart sort of injured?"

"I was." His Adam's apple bobbed. "You left me after you fed me. You are my Beloved, and you left me."

"I fed you because I could see you needed blood. But I wasn't your soul mate, if that's what you are talking about."

"How did you know I was a Dark One?" he asked, his features tight with suspicion. He sat up, and absently, I pulled a couple of pillows from where I'd slept with them, and stacked them behind his back. "How did you know I needed blood?"

"Well, for one, I figured anyone who had been blown up like you and survived couldn't have been mortal. Then when you were moaning, I caught a glimpse of your canine teeth, which were all fangy, and I figured you were a vampire."

"Dark One," he corrected, but it seemed like an automatic comment. His expression had softened a little, but his eyes were still just about shooting me with lasers. "Why did you leave me if you knew what I was?"

"I didn't really leave you, not in the sense you mean. I shouldn't have been there to begin with, because I was sick." I put a hand on his arm. His flesh was warm, the muscles underneath it as hard as banded steel. We both looked down at my hand. "You heal fast," I told him, noting that the cuts and abrasions were already fading.

"Sick? You are … what are you?" he asked with a puzzled expression.

"I told you. I'm a cartomancer. Man. You have nice arms. I like nice arms on a man. That sounds stupid, because who doesn't like nice arms? But yours are beyond nice. They are arms plus. They're solid, but not bodybuilder beefy. Not like the thief taker twins. Your arms are good. Manly. Enticing, even."

"You betrayed me. You abandoned me. You fed me, then left me to suffer untold torments. My arms don't care what you think of them. You will cease lusting after them this instant," he said with what I imagined he thought was a self-righteous mien. He ruined that completely by taking my hand in his and absently kissing my knuckles. "This is strange. Cartomancer? I have not heard of your kind."

"We're not super rare, but we're not everywhere, either," I said, scooting a bit closer to him, savoring the heat that seemed to exude from his body. I badly wanted to strip him naked, but reminded myself that he seemed to be under the delusion I'd done something cruel to him in the past, not to mention the fact that he had been wounded on the way to my room, and I had never been a "strip a near stranger naked the second I got him in my hotel room" sort of woman.

I was willing to make an exception for Ivo, however.

He was healing up very nicely, I couldn't help but notice. Even the nail bed of his pinkie finger was looking much less gruesome.

"But you claim you were ill?" He looked so rumpled and out of sorts that I couldn't help but brush back his dark hair that had fallen down over his brow, and straightened what remained of his shirt, allowing my fingers to trace down the now-uninjured length of his arm.

"Yes. I was poisoned by mustard gas. It turns out that even cartomancers are affected by that. I was recuperating at a nearby hospital when the call came in that there had been heavy action in our area, and all medical personnel were needed. So I went to help out, but I didn't last more than about sixteen hours before I collapsed. They sent me to another hospital, thinking I had pneumonia, and then shipped me back to Canada. I didn't leave you, Ivo. Not willingly, anyway. I didn't realize that by feeding you I was doing … something. I'm not quite sure what a Beloved is other than some sort of a romantic partner."

"It is, as you said, more of a soul mate." He considered me gravely, his eyes still shadowed by pain, but at least he was no longer looking at me as if I had done him wrong.

"That sounds like something people who believe in fate subscribe to," I told him gently. "I'm not in that group, just so you know. I don't let the universe boss me around. I may be a cartomancer, but I don't necessarily do what the cards advise. What happened to you after I was taken off to another hospital?"

"I died," he said.

My eyebrows rose as I made a show of inspecting his recumbent form. "You look pretty damned good for a corpse, Ivo."

"In effect I died," he said, making an abrupt gesture that ended with his hand on my bare thigh. We both looked at it for a moment. His fingers spasmed as he cleared his throat. "That is, when I realized that you had bound me to you, and I could no longer feed from others, I allowed myself to fall into a state referred to as noctambul. It allowed me to exist—barely—without going to the trouble of actually killing myself."

"I'm glad you didn't do that," I said quickly, trying to assess if he was revealing any troubling ideations of self-harm. "Just so you know, I worked for a suicide prevention organization during the nineteen seventies and eighties, so I'm perfectly happy to talk to you if you are having any feelings of despair."

"I did despair, because my Beloved abandoned me," he said, blinking impossibly long black eyelashes. His eyes were a lovely mixture of soft green and pale gray, with a dark ring on the outside of the iris. "Although now I am willing to rethink those feelings. Do you wish to have sexual congress?"

"Huh?" I asked, wondering for a moment if he could read the particularly smutty thoughts I was having at that moment. "That was a fast turnaround. One minute you're blaming me for dumping you—which I feel obligated to repeat that I did not do—and the next you want me to jump your bones?"

"I like how you speak," he said. "I never quite know what you will say. That would annoy me in others, but in you, it is intriguing. You did not answer my question."

"I know, and I like how you talk, too. You sound British, and you talk like something out of a Victorian etiquette book, but oddly enough, that's kind of a turn-on."

"Turn-on," he repeated, his eyes narrowing on me.

"It means that yes, I do wish to have sex with you, but

not if you are still hurt from your ride here, and also, we just met. I don't normally hook up with men I've just met. Although I guess we've known each other for a pretty long time, but still. Do you?"

"Wish to make love to you?" He closed his eyes for a moment, taking a long shuddering breath. "I've wanted to since you fed me."

"Dude," I said on a laugh, moving his hand that was starting to quest again, this time heading up toward my party zone. "We didn't even meet back then. You were lying in about a million pieces in a field hospital less than a mile from the front. How could you possibly want to get it on?"

"I'm male," he said just as if that explained it. "Also, the act of feeding between a Dark One and his Beloved tends to be arousing to both parties." He frowned for a moment. "Did you not feel that connection?"

"No, but to be honest, I had a fever, had difficulty breathing, and vomited frequently. It's hard to feel like sexy times when your body is trying to purge itself of all your internal organs."

"That would explain it sufficiently, yes," he said, nodding to himself, and got up from the bed.

I remained where I was sitting, watching him, wondering if he was going to strip himself and pounce. "How do you feel?" I asked.

He looked thoughtful for a few seconds. "Semiaroused. Hungry. Slightly hotter than normal, but I assume that is due to my wounds healing. Are you ready for the lines I have composed in your honor?"

"You're going to read me a poem?" I asked, draping myself over the pillows that were still warm from his body heat. It seemed to sink into my blood, making me feel restless and needy. "Right now? I just told you that I was willing to forgo my usual objection to jumping into bed with a man I just met, and you want to recite poetry?"

"Yes," he said, then with quick, efficient movements removed the remainder of his clothing, folding them neatly before placing them on the single chair the room offered.

I couldn't help but ogle the sudden exposure of a whole lot of man standing buck naked in front of me, my brain staggering to a halt while it took in the full glory of his chest.

"'Sweet bird whose song lightens my loins,'" he said, striking a pose that was similar to the one he had adopted when reading his emo poetry earlier.

"Sorry, I don't mean to interrupt," I said, changing my position so that it was more enticing. "But you said you just wrote this poem?"

"It is not a complete work, just a few lines that came to me as I was fetching Christian's motorcycle," he said, then lifted his head and stretched out his arm to emote again. "'Sweet bird whose song lightens my loins, I mournest yet for when you leave my side—'"

"Sorry again, but are you calling me a bird?" I asked, flipping over onto my belly, kicking my heels over my butt, and sending him a come-hither look.

"It is a metaphor for you, yes. It is not the way of poets to simply call the object of their attention as they are," he explained, then straightened up into his recitation pose. "'Alone do I watch the night come as day recedes.'"

"OK, but you are aware that 'bird' is slang for a woman, right? I just didn't know which way you meant it." I rolled onto my side, and arranged myself in a mermaid pose, allowing the hem of the tee to ride up a bit on my leg. Not enough to flash him, but close to it.

"'Taking with the day's bliss your hips, your legs, your breasts,'" he said in a manner that made me think he was close to grinding his teeth. He paused and glared at me. I just smiled, and smoothed a hand down the pillow. "'If thou couldst not guess how deep my sorrow—'"

"You don't hear people use the word 'couldst' enough these days," I commented, lolling back on the pillows.

He put his hands on his hips. "Do you want to hear the lines that I composed for you, or not?"

"Yes, of course I do. I'm a big supporter of the arts, literary included. I just have little experience with poetry."

I gave him a toothy smile, wondering what the hell it was going to take to get him into the bed. "Please, by all means, proceed."

"'When you hide your succulent form lest my fervent gaze caress it—'"

"How much more is there to it?" I asked. "Not that I mind if it's long, but if it is going to take a while to get through all of it, then maybe I better visit the little cartomancer's room."

"You don't want to hear this, do you?" he accused, his hands back on his naked hips.

"Of course I want to hear the poem you wrote for me," I said, sitting up again since lolling did nothing but smoosh my breasts to the side. "It would be rude of me to want to romp in the bed instead of listening to it."

He took a deep breath. I admired what that did to his chest, and thought about asking him to take a few more.

"Some would say it's rude to keep interrupting a person who is attempting to recite the lines which he, at great mental cost due to concentration, composed just for their delectation."

"See, that's exactly what I mean when I say that you talk like a Victorian poetry book. It's fun, Ivo. Sexy, even." I patted the bed. "Why don't you come here where it's comfy, and you can tell me the rest of your poem."

"No." He crossed his arms and looked pointedly grumpy at me. "You don't want to hear it."

"I do," I argued.

"You don't. That's why you keep stopping me." His hair was ruffled as if it, too, were annoyed with me, while his penis remained at half-mast. I spent a moment eyeing the latter, then moved my gaze down to his thighs.

"You know, for a man who says he's been snoozing away the last eighty-six years, you are in remarkably good shape. Exceptionally good shape, one might even say. Your thighs, for instance."

He bent to look down at them. "They are thighs."

"Yes, but they're deliciously manly. They have thick muscles on the top that I just want to touch and taste and possibly rub my breasts upon."

"'All the woes of the world are named as mine / Until you return, my true spirit will fail,'" he said, the words tumbling over each other as he leaped onto the bed next to me, and pulled me over him. "You may commence tasting, touching, and breast rubbing."

"Are you sure?" I couldn't help laughing a little at the expectant way he lay beneath me, stiff as a board except his hands, which were even now attempting to pull my T-shirt off. I clutched it for a minute, wanting to make sure that he was fine with the whole idea of intimacy. "You seem to be having emotions that I don't equate with the usual ones men feel."

"I am not a usual man, and thus, I am eclectic. I am a Dark One. You are my Beloved, one who has been withheld from me for eighty-six years. Dark Ones deprived of their Beloveds die. Thus, yes, I wish to copulate. I also wish to feed, but I will not ask that of you if you are not willing to provide for me, although again, if you withhold yourself, I will have to return to a state of noctambul."

"If Dark Ones die without their women, then why did you go to sleep, instead?" I couldn't stop from asking. I was a bit confused about how it worked and, although I badly wanted to commence rubbing myself over him, needed to have this straight before I did so.

"We were not Joined. There are seven steps to Joining. We have only performed a few of them. I believe because of that, and the fact that you only fed me once, I was able to survive your loss, although I could not feed from another."

I looked down at his eyes, now a beautiful mossy green with just hints of gray. "Wait, are you saying what I think you're saying? You want to have sex, but you don't want me to feed you?"

"Not unless you agree to do so," he answered, his hands stilling on my back. "I would survive another parting from you so long as I don't feed again. But to do so would bind me to you in ways that you may not wish to accept. It is a decision from which, for me, there is no turning back. But you have the choice. I do not. I will not feed from you unless you are willing to accept that I will require you to be an integral part of my life."

I was touched, there was no denying that. And it went a long way to making me understand the sense of desperation that seemed to leach into the air around him. He was giving me the opportunity to decide not just my future but his, as well.

"There's still a lot to unpack in what you said, but although I don't want you to fade away to nothing, I'm not willing to commit to a relationship yet, because we really don't know each other."

"I understand," he said, and for a second, I felt like weeping. I wasn't sure where these emotions were coming from, but I suspected that just being near him was triggering something deep in me that had been missing for my entire life. "I would never force you to do anything you did not wish to do, including binding yourself to me. Do you still wish to rub yourself on my thighs?"

"Oh, hell, yes," I said, wiggling against him. "My body very much wants to get to know your body better."

"Excellent. We will proceed with that," he said, whipping my T-shirt off me, his hands going wild as he took my breasts immediately into them. They were pleased with this situation, and when he gently rubbed his thumbs over my nipples, I arched into them, my breath catching in my throat. "You have much more splendid breasts than I imagined on my ride here. I will have to compose a few lines specifically for them."

"If you keep touching me like that, I may have to write you a poem of appreciation, also. Jeezumcrow, Ivo. Your chest is so enticing. Do you like your nipples played with, too?"

He stopped nuzzling his cheek—thankfully now healed, although it did feel a bit warm—on the underside of my breasts. "I don't know. No woman has ever tried to—fwah!"

I had leaned down while he spoke, and took one manly nipple nub in my mouth, swirling my tongue around it before scraping it gently, oh so gently, between my teeth.

The next thing I knew, I was on my back with Ivo looming over me, his hair standing on end, his penis no longer undecided as to what it wanted to do. It was fully on board with the seduction plan, and poked me on the thigh as Ivo repeated the teeth-on-nipple act on me.

"Oh, goddess, yes," I said on a moan, clutching the sheet beneath me as his tongue joined the fun, teasing and tormenting first one breast, then the other. "You may have been asleep for eighty-six years, but damn, sir! You are really good at breast tormenting."

"You smell so good," he murmured, kissing a path down my breastbone to my belly. "Your scent fills my senses. It burns in my blood, driving me to the very edge of sanity. It binds me with ethereal chains of desire. It brings out the primal man in me. I want to claim you. Mark you as mine. Possess you as moonlight possesses the night."

"You poetic Victorian vampire, you," I said on a near growl. "I'm so not into men dominating women, but holy handbells, Ivo. You saying things like you want to claim me just makes me want to … I don't know … claim you, too."

"We shall claim each other equally," he said, his breath steaming a spot on my hip. He hesitated for a few seconds, time I used by tracing my fingers along the planes of his chest and arms. Even the red puckered skin that resulted from his wounds closing had faded away, leaving his skin unblemished and silky smooth.

I wiggled my hips a little, wondering why he appeared to be fixated at the spot on my hip. And that's when I realized that the arms braced next to me that I had been stroking weren't rigid because he was supporting himself, but that he was locked in some sort of an internal battle.

"Ivo?"

He didn't answer. His head was turned away from me, but I could see the cords of his neck standing out in stark relief.

I scooted myself down until I was directly under him. His eyes were screwed shut, his jaw tight, his lips a barely visible thin line.

"Are you all right? Did you hurt something internally? If you tell me what the pain feels like—"

"No," he managed to say, turning his head to face me, his eyes open and blazing with a deep, consuming need that rolled off him in palpable waves. "It's not that."

"It's me, isn't it?" I asked him, wanting to touch him, but unsure of his reaction if I did so.

"Yes. I thought I could do this. I want to do this. I want to pleasure you."

"But you can't without feeding?"

He moved off me, lying on his back, one hand rubbing his face. "I should be able to. Other Dark Ones can. But when I get close to you, when the taste and feel of you fills my senses, then …" He stopped, turning his face away.

I said nothing. I didn't know what I could say to comfort him. I knew what he was trying to do, how he was giving me the opportunity to decide whether I wanted to join my life with his, but my emotions were too tangled to make such a life-altering decision.

Especially not in the heat of full-body lust.

"I'm sorry," I finally said.

He nodded, obviously understanding all that I didn't say.

"Do you want me to—" I gestured toward his penis, which was still looking hopeful. "Finish you off?"

He turned to look at me at that. "You'd do that?"

"Yes. I'm not saying I'd make the same offer to anyone else, because … well, we both participated, so your sexual arousal isn't my problem. But I like you, Ivo. And much as I'd like to do things together, I would also enjoy giving you pleasure, if you could stand that without it pushing you past what's bearable.

We both considered his penis for a few seconds.

"Would you allow me to reciprocate?" he asked, his eyes glittering with an emotion I couldn't read.

"Could you do that without … you know … going into bitey mode?"

His gaze dropped to my breasts, then hips. Without answering, he got off the bed and, with short, efficient movements, donned his clothing and one shoe. I winced when he fought to force the zipper on his jeans. "It's better if I leave," he said finally, pausing at the door to cast a glance back at me.

I swear I could feel his gaze on my naked self as if he were touching me with velvet.

"Are you going to be all right?" I asked.

He was silent for a few seconds. "I have survived much before. I will do so again."

"I hate to say—the motorcycle—I don't want you to hurt yourself again—" I stopped, my heart weeping for the despair that I could feel wrapping itself around him.

"I'll walk back," was all he said. The door made a soft swooshing noise as it closed behind him.

I lay in bed for about half an hour while I picked through my thoughts and emotions, and the growing sense that I had made a choice I would regret to the end of my days.

"Don't be silly," I told myself as I got out of bed. I couldn't stand to lie there, the faintest hints of Ivo's scent lingering on the linens. It did something to me, that scent. I understood what he meant about it permeating his being. It felt to me as if it was sinking into my body, merging with me, making me something new and exciting. "You're just reacting to the neediness of his situation. You're not thinking sensibly. If you do what you want to do, you're going to be tied to him forever. That's how vampires work."

The face that stared back at me from the mirror looked like a stranger's, her expression stricken, her eyes haunted. I touched my face, wondering how much I'd changed since 1916.

My body was much the same, although I bore a few scars from the times I'd been injured. But my psyche, my sense of self … had that changed?

"Yes," I told the stranger in the mirror. "Minerva in 1916 would have gladly stayed with Ivo. But my life is much different now. I have …" I stopped. I've never been able to lie to myself. It's something to do with my cartomancy self being forced to say what I see in the cards.

"I have a life," I finished, moving over to the radiator. My underwear was still slightly damp, but I pulled it on nonetheless. The bra was still not dry, so I left it.

"I have friends." I gathered up my clothes and shoes, putting them on without thinking. "My life has meaning."

I straightened up the sheets and duvet. "I may not have a job or even a change of clothes, but I am not a wandering empty soul drifting through life looking for a man to complete me. I am sufficient unto myself."

The pillow I held in my hand smelled like Ivo. I buried my face in it for a second, then stopped fighting it.

"I'm his Beloved," I told the woman in the mirror as I slipped the room key into my pocket. "But more importantly, he needs me. So you can stop looking at me like I'm desperate for a bit of nooky, and be impressed by the fact that I'm committing myself to making sure he doesn't ever look sad like he did when he left. Or be alone without anyone to take care of him. Or let him ride that damned motorcycle until he gets some lessons under his belt."

Tears filled my eyes as I spoke, but I brushed them away angrily, unsure of why I felt so emotional. Then I went to the hotel lobby and convinced a couple outside to give me a ride back to the GothFaire.

FIVE

"Has the door to my mausoleum been repaired?" Ivo asked when he entered Christian's castle. Finch sat at a desk with a device that he had informed Ivo earlier was called a laptop.

"There you are. I wondered where you'd gone off to. I thought we were going to visit the Faire together?" Finch asked.

"You were busy. I went without you. I met ..." He stopped, not wanting to go into the details of just how hellish his already nightmarish life had become. "Christian's motorcycle is in the town, at the hotel."

"It is?" Finch asked, sitting back, giving him a quizzical look, one that was oddly piercing. It made Ivo pleased that he had returned to the room given to him and utilized the fresh clothing that Finch and Christian had put at his disposal. The journey to see Minerva had left him looking less like a Dark One and more like something found squashed in a trash bin in a particularly unsavory alley. "You took it out for a ride?"

"Yes." He made no further comment about the fact that he had not mastered the machinery. If he had a future, he might do so, but what use would such knowledge be to him now? "The mausoleum door?"

"It's not yet repaired. Christian said he'd have workmen

attend to it on Monday. Are you desperately hungry? You might be able to handle a bit more pig's blood—"

"No to both," Ivo said, squaring his shoulders as he turned and left the library. He'd just have to exist until the door could be replaced. Once in his room, he paced the floor, making and discarding plans. He would not blame Minerva for her refusal to be what he needed her to be—he might be viewed in this modern time as dated in his sensibilities, but the idea of forcing her into a situation not only made his flesh crawl; it made him want to rage. No one, not even he, could be allowed to put her in a position where she had no choice in her life.

However, she was his Beloved. He owed it to her to make sure that her life would be one of as much happiness and contentment as he could provide. Therefore, he would see the two strongmen in the morning, and ascertain details about this spell that they believed Minerva had. He would then speak to her calmly, and without any of the pesky emotions, needs, and desires that roiled around inside of him, and do whatever it took to resolve the situation.

Once she was free of the strongmen's attention, he would consult a lawyer and banker, and make sure that she was given the fruit of his estate. He wasn't an overly rich man, but he had been prudent in his investments over the last two centuries, and assuming the money he had left behind in 1916 had not suffered a catastrophe, she should have enough money to live a life of comfort without having to seek employment with men such as the one who thrust her into this situation.

He nodded to himself as he removed his borrowed clothing, lying on the bed, trying very hard not to dwell on the memory of the sensations when Minerva touched him.

No, he would not think of what he couldn't have. He would be noble. He would martyr himself at her feet to ensure she had the life she sought. He would fade into the past, and soon become nothing more than a wispy image in her most distant memory.

He made a few mental notes about a particularly heart-wrenching poem depicting his noble sacrifice, and drifted to sleep trying very hard not to remember her breasts.

The dream roared to life with a ferocity that took him by surprise. One moment he was drifting on slumber's arms, and the next, he was plunged into a dream where Minerva, naked and warm, and smelling like sunlight on summer grass, was nibbling her way up his legs. He moaned at the sensation of her fingernails as they lightly scraped the sensitive flesh of his inner thighs, the cool sweep of her hair tangling on his penis, which had become almost instantly aroused. The torment continued on his belly and sides, awareness pulling at him, but he fought it, desperately wanting to remain in the dream, where all his fantasies regarding Minerva could be enacted.

"Boy, you sure are a sound sleeper. I don't suppose you'd like to wake up?" A kiss was pressed to his rib cage, stirring the hunger into life until it swept over him like a red wave. "Ivo? You're moaning, so I know you're in there. This would be a lot more fun if you were awake. Plus I don't want to do anything that you wouldn't like."

Panicked, he clung to the fragments of sleep, not wanting to give up the dream version of Minerva.

"Ivo." Pain flared briefly to life on his side, just as if an irritated woman had pinched him. With a profound sense of martyrdom, he gave up and opened his eyes, intending to make notes on just how horrible his life had become, but at that moment he realized a black shape loomed above him.

Without thinking, he grabbed the attacker, and was about to fling him across the room when he heard the pained intake of breath.

"Minerva?" he asked, squinting in the near complete blackness of the room.

"Yes. Could you—thank you."

He released his hold on her arms and switched on a bedside lamp to find Minerva straddling one of his knees. "Sorry I startled you. I thought you'd wake up when I started teasing your legs, but you just kind of twitched and moaned."

"I was dreaming," he explained, rubbing his face, as if that would clear the mental sleep fog that slowly evaporated. "You're here."

"I am," she agreed.

"How did you find me? How did you get into the castle?"

"I knocked at the door, and a nice man opened it, and I told him I wanted to see you, and he asked if I knew you, and I said yes, and then he kind of sniffed the air around me like he thought I might smell like booze, and then he stared at me for about ten seconds until I asked if I could come in because it's chilly out, and he said yes, and then showed me where your room was."

Ivo's mind was trying to sort out many things, not the least of which was why Minerva had come to him.

She patted his thigh, and continued. "I want badly to do all sorts of things to you, but I thought it would be best if you were awake. For one, I'm a huge believer in consent, and for another, it's much more fun if you get to participate. Do you want to participate, Ivo?"

"Yes," he answered without thinking. "No. That is, I want to, but I can't. Not without—"

She moved, crawling up his body until she wrapped both arms around his head. "About that. I've had a change of mind. You need me, Ivo Zeman. You really need me. Not just a woman, not a sexual partner, not a source of blood—you need me, and only me."

He stared at her in mingled hope and astonishment. Was she saying what he thought she was saying? Or had he slipped into insanity while he was sleeping? "What happened?"

"To me?" She gave a little shrug. "I think it was the realization that I was worried about you. I didn't like you going off to be alone and lonely and not cared for. And then I thought about what it would be like to go on with my life knowing you were in the world, but not with me, not reciting your really ... distinct ... poetry that you wrote just for my thighs. I have a good life, Ivo. But I think that with you, our lives will be perfectly splendid. So go ahead, the diner is open."

Ivo didn't know what to do. He was torn between wanting to dance, sing, shout from the highest of Christian's turrets that he had a Beloved, a real Beloved, one who wanted to be with him, and make love to her in a way that would leave them both as wrung out as a well-used rag.

"I choose the sexual congress," he said, pulling her down so that he could possess himself of her mouth.

She laughed a little as she kissed him back, both their hands busy divesting her of her garments until she sprawled across him naked, her flesh warm and soft and satiny where it touched his. "I like how you think. Would you mind if we skipped the foreplay? I'm still a bit revved up from earlier this evening, and my body is being obstinate about getting down to business."

"Madam," he said in his best formal voice, pausing to moan when she bent to swirl her tongue around his nipples. "You seem to be under the impression that you are in charge of the proceedings. I am the Dark One. We are naturally dominant. You, as a woman, must assume the submissive role—Christ!"

Minerva shifted to straddle his hips, her hands on his penis as she positioned him. "Sir, you are mistaken if you think that I, a mere woman, am going to stand for that complete and utter bullshit. Since I am on top, I get to be the one calling the shots. Do you like this?"

He bucked beneath her when she reached back and toyed with his testicles. It took him a minute to uncross his eyes and remember how to speak, but when he did, all that emerged from his mouth was intermittent panting accompanied by several groans of sheer pleasure.

"Good," she said, smiling as she slowly started to sink down on him. The smile changed to a look of sexual pleasure as she rocked her hips "Goddess above and below, Ivo. You are seriously endowed in the penis department. And you're so hot. I'm not sure—"

He made a hip swivel that had her eyes opening wide as her breath caught.

"Oh, yes! Do that again!" she demanded, her muscles tightening around him.

He swiveled again, his hands on her breasts, sliding around to her ass when she leaned down to kiss him. The hunger had him in its sharp red grip, but this time, he didn't have to fight it. With a profound murmur of thanks when she tipped her head, allowing him access to her neck and shoulder, he flexed his hips in time to her movements on top of him.

"Are you certain?" he managed to ask, every atom of his being screaming at him to claim her, and make her irrevocably his.

"Yes," she answered, and then gently bit the top of his shoulder.

He froze for a second—then it was all too much. His movements went choppy and wild even as her inner muscles rippled around him as she found her climax. He bit the spot where her neck joined her shoulder, his mind full of a sensation that he could describe only as rapture, his body both giving and taking life from her.

And when they finally could breathe again, he wrapped his arms around her, jerking up the duvet, keeping her safely tucked up against his side, his body, soul, and mind at peace for the first time in eighty-six years.

The argument started approximately six hours later.

"You are my Beloved," Ivo said, his arms crossed as he tried to show her that his word was law.

"I know what I am, and don't you make me regret my decision to accept the job," she told him, tsking when she pulled on her clothing. "Damn, I really wish I could get my suitcase from the cops. I'm getting tired of wearing the same outfit. I don't suppose you have any women's clothing lying around not being used?"

"We will purchase clothing for you," he said. "We will go into the town and buy you whatever you need."

"I just got done telling you that I have to go work. I told Dominic that I'd do the morning shift today, and I can't leave them in the lurch. Besides, it's good money. I made the equivalent of a couple hundred dollars yesterday. Ugh. I guess my undies are OK, but that's the first thing I'm going to buy."

"You are my Beloved," he repeated, frowning when she refused to take notice of the fact that he was being dominant and stern and unyielding. "You do not need to work. I have sufficient funds to provide for both of us."

"Goody for you, but if you think I'm a gold digger, you have another thing to think about. Do you see my shoes anywhere?" She stood in the middle of the room, glancing around. "I'm not saying it won't be nice not having to live paycheck to paycheck, but I'm not going to give up cartomancy just because you are loaded. Oh, there they are."

"Beloveds must follow the dictates of their Dark One," he said, shifting tactics since the arm-crossing and immovable stance didn't seem to make an impression on her. He'd apply to her reason, instead. "It is the way of things."

"Uh-huh." She sat on the bed and put on her shoes, sliding a glance up at him. "Ivo, I like you. I think I could easily fall in love with you, but there is no way in hell that I'm going to put up with you being Mr. Bossy, OK? Either we do this as a partnership, or we don't do this."

"We are bound together now," he pointed out, feeling the control slipping through his fingers. Minerva made him feel utterly at sea, and he didn't know what to do about it. He would die before he did anything that made her unhappy, but at the same time, she had to realize that now she had him to protect her.

"Yeah? Well, I'm willing to bet a stake through the heart could end that," she said with a pointed look at his chest that made him take a step back, indignantly rubbing a spot where he could swear he felt her gaze centered.

"You will find that Dark Ones are harder to kill than a mere stake in the heart," he said firmly as she opened the door and marched out. "Minerva! I forbid you to leave when I am telling you the way of things!"

"I don't take well to being forbidden anything, Ivo," she called back as he followed. "The sooner you learn that, the happier we'll be. Crap. How do you get out of here? Your friend brought me to your room last night, and I couldn't see the path he took."

He hurried up until he could take her arm, turning her to the left when she was going to take a right. "Was it Finch or his uncle whom you met last night?"

"No clue. He was nice, whoever he was. He didn't say much, just took me to your room."

They descended to the ground floor, entering the main hall. Finch emerged from the library looking tired, evidently having worked all night.

"Finch, you have met my Beloved?" Ivo asked, guiding Minerva to him.

"I what?" Finch stopped rubbing the back of his head and stared in surprise at them both. "Your Beloved? The one we hunted for?"

Ivo made the introductions, beaming with pride at Minerva as she greeted his friend. "She was ill with the mortals' mustard gas. That's why we didn't find her."

"You're the woman at the GothFaire," Finch said, giving her a little bow. "I've seen you there. Does Christian know?"

"I do, and I'm delighted that things worked out as they did," Christian said from a side hall, emerging to greet Minerva. "It reminds those of us who have not yet found our Beloveds that even in a dire situation like the one in which Ivo found himself, all hope is not lost. You are welcome at Drahanská, Minerva. There is no rush to leave, since there must be a great deal for Ivo to do."

"Thank you, but as I was just telling Mr. Bossy here, I have to run or I'll be late for morning shift at the Goth-Faire." She slid her hand from Ivo's, giving him a long look that he felt was unusually full of barbed warnings, then, with a nod at Finch and Christian, hurried out of the hall.

"Mr. Bossy?" Finch asked, his eyebrows raised.

"She is a bit overwhelmed by becoming my Beloved in deed as well as in name," Ivo tried to explain, but he could have sworn that Christian's cough following that statement had a hint of laughter to it. "She has lived amongst mortals for a long time, I believe, and thus feels an obligation to them. Naturally, that will change now that I am here to protect and guide her."

"*Guide,*" Christian repeated, then had another coughing fit.

Finch nodded. "Yes, that's a good idea. She clearly needs to be taught what it is to be a Beloved. Well, I am for bed unless you need me. Oh, Ivo, one of the groundsmen brought back Christian's Harley. Did you have problems with it?"

"Not really. It is just a bit different, not quite what I'm used to." Ivo pulled the tablet from his inner coat pocket. "Perhaps I will ride it later, but first, I must contact my bankers to release funds. Then there are decisions to be made about our future."

"You might want to consult Minerva before you make those decisions," Christian said, his lips oddly stiff.

Ivo eyed his friend's uncle, wondering if he was having some sort of mouth spasm. "Naturally, I will take her wishes into consideration. But she is a woman. She has been alone, yes, but now she has me to take charge of her life and see to her comforts."

Christian nodded, and made an odd choking sound as he turned away, his shoulders shaking.

Finch climbed the stairs to get a few hours' sleep. Ivo availed himself of the telephone in Christian's library, making several calls after using his tablet to find the information he needed.

Thus it was that two hours had passed before he emerged from the castle, one of Christian's brown leather fedoras on his head to shade him from the weak autumn sun. It was a short stroll down to the north meadow, and thence to the small poetry stage that was located next to where Minerva read cards.

"The fire in your eye lights the cold embers of my soul," he said as he strode toward the area, mentally composing a few lines of praise for Minerva, since she obviously loved his poetry. He looked forward to providing her a lifetime of such treats. *"And your breasts delight my heart, my mind, my thighs* … blast. Where is she?"

"Hello. Are you here for the poetry—oh, it's you again." The woman who had appeared yesterday with a clipboard looked pleased to see him. "Excellent. We haven't had much action, so if you'd like to take the stage—"

"Another time, I would be happy to. But I am looking for Minerva," he told her, his gaze straying to the stage. He would very much like to recite his second-best poem, but Minerva would undoubtedly wish to be there to hear it.

"Who? Oh, the card reader? You just missed her. She went off with a couple of big bulldogs."

"Dogs? She has dogs?" He searched his memory, but didn't recall her mentioning that she had dogs. He wished she had—he was very fond of animals, and would have liked to meet hers.

"No, not those sorts of bulldogs. The human kind, with no necks, and squinty little eyes. I think they were Austrian."

For a moment, Ivo could have sworn that his blood had turned to ice; then he was running, racing away from the Faire, his mind focused on one horrifying thought—the strongmen who sought Minerva had finally found her. What did she call them? Thief takers? "No one touches my Beloved," he ground between his teeth as he dashed into the stable block that served as a garage, and a minute later spun an arc of rocks as Christian's motorcycle leaped between his legs, the roar of the engine almost as loud as the chant that was currently filling his head. *Not now that I just found her, not now that I just found her* …

He wasn't aware of anything as he drove down the hill, the Faire and stages a blur as the wind whipped tears from his eyes, his fingers white where they gripped the handlebars. Ahead, he saw a panel van turning from the small town onto a road that no doubt led to Brno. There was very little traffic leaving the town; most of it was pouring into the fields set aside for festival parking.

Ivo hunched low as he remembered how to shift, sending the motorcycle rocketing forward at a speed that left everything a blur except the white van.

By the time he caught up with it, his face was grimy with dirt, his eyes streamed nonstop, and his fingers hurt with the strength of his grip. He swung out around the van, narrowly missed smashing himself on the front of an oncoming automobile, and had only a glimpse of startled faces in the van before he pulled in front of it, spinning the motorcycle around with an unearthly scream of tires that was echoed when the driver of the van slammed on his brakes. The van fishtailed as Ivo remained still in the middle of the road, one foot on the ground, watching as the van took out a signpost before coming to a shuddering halt.

Then he was off the motorcycle, jerking open the driver's door and pulling one of the strongmen out of the seat.

"What the—" the man squawked, but Ivo had no time for explanations. He simply ripped away a flat black belt that crossed the man's chest, and pulled the man from the van before flinging him over the verge, where he rolled down an incline to soggy pastureland.

"Minerva!" he yelled, leaping into the van, twisting in order to land a kick on the second strongman, who was trying to unbuckle another chest belt. His foot connected with the man's jaw, snapping his head back with enough force to crack the glass of the window.

"Mmrph!"

He lunged past the man to the dimness of the van, his heart beating madly as he grabbed the flailing form barely visible.

"I found you!" He held the struggling form to his chest for a few seconds, breathing deeply of her, ignoring the unpleasant scents of oil and mud and rust from the interior, and glorying in the fact that his Beloved, his Minerva, was alive and well, and had not been taken from him. "Are you well, sweet? Did they harm you? If they did, I will see to it that they never harm another."

The thug in the front began to groggily swear in German, shaking his head in a manner that sprayed blood all over the front of the window.

"Never fear, I will see to it that no further harm comes to you," he promised the oddly twitching form of Minerva. It struck him then that she was also unusually quiet, emitting only assorted grunts. He decided that it would be best to remove her from the van so that he could attend to any hurt she had suffered by the kidnapping. Then he would punish the strongmen. "Come, let us leave. I will attend to you in a safer location."

A dull rumbling sound could be heard from the other side of the van as Ivo yanked open the side door, and emerged from it with Minerva in his arms. Honking from in front of him drew his attention momentarily. He glared at an auto that was clearly upset with his motorcycle being parked in the middle of the road, and said loudly, "My Beloved has been injured. Cease making that noise so that I might see to her. Then I will move the motorcycle."

"Mmrrr!"

Ivo glanced down at Minerva as he gently carried her to the grassy verge. He was momentarily startled to see a wide silver tape covering her mouth, her eyes all but spitting anger at him. "Sweet?" he asked as he set her on her feet. "What is this?"

"MMR!" she said, hopping up and down. He peered behind her and noted that her hands had been bound with a narrow bit of white cording that poked out stiffly. Nothing about her seemed to indicate that she was injured, however, which allowed him to take the first full breath since the Faire woman had told him she'd been taken. "MMMH!"

"Yes. I see. You are uncomfortable. I will remove your bindings. ..." He patted his pockets as if he was expecting to find a knife. "Unfortunately, I did not know I would be called upon to cut anything today, so I don't have anything sharp upon me," he told her.

She stamped her foot, drew her eyebrows together, then stomped hard on *his* foot.

"Beloved!" he said, hopping up and down on one leg for a moment, before turning to face the automobile that was continuing to honk at him. "Stop that noise! I am trying to reason with my Beloved, and I can't do that if you are making that ruckus. Now, Minerva—"

She tried to kick him. When he moved aside in time to avoid the blow, she responded with a growl behind her gag.

"I'm trying," he told her, holding up his hands. "But as you can see, I have nothing with which to remove your bindings."

She bent double and would have slammed her head in his belly in what was obviously an attack, but he caught her by the shoulders, and spun her around, moving her over to the motorcycle. He noted absently that the strongman in the field was sitting up and rubbing his head. "Yes, yes, my love, but now is not the time to play. Let us go to Christian's castle, where he is sure to have a knife we can use. Can you mount the machine behind me?"

She appeared to scream, and jumped up and down a few more times before it struck him what her objection was.

"Ah. I see your point. You wish for this to be removed. It appears to be adhered to your skin. Very well, I will remove it quickly. You might wish to brace yourself," he said, picking at a corner of the silver adhesive. "Ready?"

"Mmr—aaaaaaaaaaieeeeeeeeee!"

He pulled the adhesive quickly. Minerva stood frozen for a second, her eyes wide; then she screamed at the top of her lungs.

"You bloody boob! You great big bloodsucking boob of a man! Holy hellballs, that hurts!"

The flesh around her lips appeared red and angry. Not knowing what else to do, he pressed kisses to it, feathering them lightly in case the skin was tender.

"You could have eased it off, you know. You could have gotten some baby oil or something to work it up. You didn't have to just rip it right … off … like … oh, Ivo." She swooned against him, her mouth parting in invitation. He didn't refuse it, giving her a kiss to let her know just how worried he'd been.

"Hey!"

"If you think a few kisses is going to get you off the hook for yanking duct tape off my face, you're so very wrong," she told him, but the corners of her mouth curled, her eyes smoky with desire.

"Hey, you!"

"I love you," he told her, surprised by the words at the same time that he knew them to be absolutely, completely, irrevocably true.

She blinked twice. "You do?"

"Hey, you can't do that. Ow. I think my arm is broken. Hey!" The first strongman staggered toward them.

"I do. I don't suppose you've fallen in love with me yet?"

To his annoyance, she pursed her lips and looked thoughtful. "I'm not sure. It's hard to pinpoint my emotions when the lower half of my face is on fire, and my wrists hurt because they are zip-tied behind me."

"Would it help if I licked your face?" he asked.

"Ew. No. I mean, I don't mind a little licking. That can be sexy. But my face? My whole face?"

"I meant the wounded areas. Dark Ones have an enzyme in their saliva that acts as a coagulant. It might help ease the redness."

"It *is* broken! Look, I can't even make a fist." The strongman waved his arm in the air.

"That bullyboy is coming," Minerva said, her lips quirked in another slight smile. "We should probably go."

"Yes. Get on the machine behind me. We'll go find something to cut your bindings."

"I'm not getting on behind you. I can't hold on to you. I'll fall off. Not to mention the fact that I'm not letting you drive me around on that thing. Not when you can't even go a couple of miles without getting road rash all over you and losing fingernails hither and yon."

"It's growing back, and the injuries were mostly confined to just my left side. Also, I made it here without so much as a scratch," he pointed out with dignity.

"Uh-huh." She tipped her head up. "You have a smashed bug on your forehead. Will you shut it?"

Ivo was momentarily taken aback until he realized she was yelling the last sentence at the person driving the auto. There were several more behind them now.

"How am I going to do my job when I can't even make a fist?" the strongman strode through waist-high grass, approaching the road.

"Gurg!" came an answering statement from inside the van. "Hurt. Ow."

"Get on in front of me," Ivo told Minerva, and after she said something extremely profane to the driver who kept honking at them, she did so.

The motorcycle roared to life, drowning out the cries of the strongman who was trying to get to the road.

"I swear, though, that if you kill me on this damned bike, I will haunt you to the end of your days, making sure that each and every one of them is the pinnacle of abject misery," Minerva promised. "Just you remember that, Ivo. Abject misery to the end of time!"

He couldn't be more in love.

SIX

Ivo's buddy Finch emerged from the castle just as we pulled up at an adjacent outbuilding.

He did a double take, stared for a few seconds, then approached us carefully as Ivo turned off the motorcycle. "What ... erm ... what happened to you?"

"This man," I said, aware that my voice was emerging in a near snarl, but unable to keep it from being such, "this man is not allowed to use a motorcycle again. Do you understand? He is a danger to not only himself, but others, as well."

"Ignore my Beloved," Ivo said, attempting to help me off the saddle of the bike. I thought about kicking him, but decided that was conduct unbecoming in a cartomancer. "She is a bit distraught."

"A bit distraught?" I damned my cartomancer reputation and swung my leg over the handlebars, kicking at him. Damn his nimble hide, he managed to step out of the way before my foot connected with his kneecap. "A bit distraught? Is that what you call almost being killed multiple times during a four-mile drive? A bit distraught, Ivo?"

Finch's gaze moved from me to Ivo and back again. "There was trouble?"

I took a deep, deep breath. "You could call it that," I said at the exact moment that Ivo answered, "None at all. Minerva is distressed because I was unable to remove the binding from her face without causing her pain, and also, her hands are bound with a material that I was unable to break without hurting her wrists."

"Do you have a knife?" I asked Finch, shooting a potent glare at Ivo, which he blandly ignored.

"Yes." He pulled out a small folding pocketknife, handing it to Ivo. "You'll forgive me for asking, but why have you strapped Ivo's shirt about your torso? Also, what happened to his trousers?"

"Both very good questions. I can answer them with one word: Ivo."

"There was another slight contretemps with the machine," Ivo explained, cutting the zip tie off my wrists. The only reason I didn't punch him in the chest as he deserved was that he took my hands in his, and gently massaged the red marks where the ties had cut into my flesh. "I believe it was due to the fact that Minerva rode in front of me. It offset the motorcycle, causing it to fall repeatedly."

I pointed at him. "The reason that I am not at this moment divorcing you is the fact that each of the three times that you crashed us, you managed to twist yourself around me so that I wasn't the one who hit the road, the grass verge, and that poor cow who was minding her own business in a pasture a good hundred feet off the road."

Finch looked at Ivo with what I could only interpret as admiration. "You hit a cow in a field?"

"It was not as dire as Minerva makes it seem," Ivo said, waving away the fact that he was nothing short of a maniac on a motorcycle. "She had shifted on the seat, and the motorcycle went off the road and into an open pasture. The cow was unharmed, once we got her back onto her feet. Unfortunately, she disliked the machine, and Minerva got tangled on her horns, tearing her shirt. Naturally, I had to give her mine."

"And your trousers?" Finch asked. All three of us looked at Ivo's legs. I was just thankful he was wearing underwear.

"That would be the pond outside of town," he said, clearing his throat and looking into the distance, as if trying hard to pretend the conversation wasn't happening.

"The motorcycle bucked him off into the pond," I told Finch. "I managed to land on the grass, but Ivo rolled down into the water."

"Pond?" Finch frowned. "I don't think I know of a pond in town. There's a cesspit that is in the process of being drained ... oh."

"Yes. We noticed the smell, hence the removal of his jeans." I looked at the man with whom, despite the sane part of my mind's warnings, I was infatuated to the point that I knew it wouldn't take much more for me to be fully and wholly in love. "I don't suppose there are any spare women's clothes in your uncle's castle? I don't have anything else to wear, and I really need to get back to the Faire."

"I believe so. I will ask my uncle's housekeeper, Eve," Finch told me, and turned on his heel to reenter the house.

"Beloved!" Ivo said in that bossy tone he liked to take with me. It amused me to see how hard he tried to be firm and un-yielding, and yet the instant that he thought I was unhappy, he was moving heaven and earth to please me. "I can't allow that. The strongmen might return to capture you again."

I slid a bit further toward love at the memory of how well he'd protected me each time he'd crashed. And then there was the heroic way he'd saved me from the kidnappers. ... I sighed to myself. Why was I even trying to make sense of it? I loved him despite his horrendous poetry, Victorian sensibilities, and dismal ability at riding a motorcycle.

"Actually, I kind of hope they try, although I don't want them to succeed," I told him, rubbing my wrists. "Did it ever occur to you to wonder why they kidnapped me?"

"Of course it occurred to me," he said in a manner that indicated that it hadn't, until that moment, done so. "Obvi-ously it must be related to this spell that your employer has stolen."

"On the nose," I said, booping him on his before taking his hand and leading him into the castle. "They were taking me to see Jason. I wanted to know why, but they wouldn't say, just that this was what their boss wanted. Oh, thank you."

A woman with stark black hair with a side stripe of white bustled up to me, speaking softly in Czech, offering me an armful of garments.

I quickly picked out a couple of skirts that looked like they would fit, as well as three shirts, and a pair of leggings that would probably be a bit too short but would be nice under the big fisherman's sweater that I included after the memory of the chilly wind during the ride back to the castle.

Eve the housekeeper didn't so much as raise an eyebrow at the sight of Ivo standing in nothing but his underwear, but accepted my thanks with a nod of her head, and retreated into one of the many dark hallways that led off the main entrance.

"If you insist on returning to the Faire despite my wishes for you to remain safe, so that we can have a long and happy life together rather than you being killed by the two clearly deranged strongmen, which would result in my almost immediate death, then I will accompany you," Ivo informed me ten minutes later when I had a quick wash in his bathroom, donned the leggings and one of the lightweight sweaters, and filched one of Ivo's plaid wool shirts to tie around my waist in case it got too cold while I finished my interrupted shift. He was once again clad in jeans and a black wool shirt that set off his eyes in a way that made my stomach squirm with happiness.

I gave him a long look. "You're writing a poem about the kidnapping and your subsequent rescue of me right now, aren't you?"

"Yes," he said, trying to look down his nose at me before herding me out of the room and down the stairs. "I am, as I have mentioned, a poet. It is what I do. Besides, you love my poems."

I shot him a startled glance, but rather than telling him the truth, a strange determination rose within me. I made a promise to myself right then that I would not tolerate anyone bad-mouthing his literary output. He might be a horrible poet, but he was *my* horrible poet, and I would not have his feelings hurt for anything. "All right, but you can't scare away any potential customers. I still have two hours to go."

"Will you read cards for me again if I pay you?" he asked as we walked hand in hand past the main stage, where a trio was crooning out ballads.

"I will happily read your cards, but you don't have to pay me for it." I smiled when I saw four people milling around the upturned wooden box from which my sign still fluttered. "Just let me take care of these people first, OK?"

It took more than an hour before I had time to get to Ivo's reading. He spent the time sitting on the edge of the small poetry slam stage alternately looking thoughtful and tapping on the tablet that he treated like his most precious possession.

He was writing more poetry about me, I just knew he was.

"Right, let's see what the cards want you to know," I told him, quickly shuffling, and having him cut them before I laid out five in a line. "I think we'll forgo the detailed spreads and do a quick and dirty read."

"That doesn't look good," he said, pointing at the Devil card.

"Eh. It's not as bad as ... oh." I laid out a Broken Tower card next to it. "Yeah. OK. Let's start from the left. First card, king of cups. This tells me that you are a giving person, that you get what you want by helping others. Incidentally, it's also a card that says you need to let go of the past, but I think that at this point, that's a given. Second card is seven of swords."

"I enjoy fencing," Ivo said, peering at the card. He squinted just a little.

"That's good to know. Are you by any chance shortsighted?" I asked. "I apologize if that sounds rude. I don't know if vampires can have bad vision or not."

"It's not rude, and I am, as a matter of fact." His expression went guarded. "Does that bother you?"

"No! Far from it. I've noticed you squinting a few times, and I couldn't tell if it was just a habit, or if you couldn't see well."

"My spectacles were lost during the battle where I was blown up. I didn't have them replaced before I went into noctambul."

"Gotcha. We'll get you a new pair of glasses as soon as possible. It can't be fun not being able to see well. Back to the seven of swords. Swords are a suit that talks about difficulties and the actions taken to overcome them. And seven cards are mostly about not giving up a fight. So this card tells you that there is deception around you, but you need to think on your feet in order to emerge victorious."

"That could be the strongmen," he said, glancing behind him.

"Possibly. This is the queen of cups. She's here to tell you to listen to your heart."

"You may tell her that I have done so," he said with a look so heated that I almost fanned myself despite the coolness of the day.

I smiled, and blew him a kiss. "OK, let's get to these two cards. The Devil and the Tower cards are warnings. The Devil warns you against falling into addictive behaviors and giving in to temptation, including patterns of negative thoughts."

"I spent eighty-six years in that state," he said, his lips thinning. I put my hand on his, wanting to offer him comfort, but not knowing how I could erase the pain of all those years. "Do not, Beloved," he said, lifting my hand to kiss my fingers.

"Don't what?"

"Feel guilty. Our past may have been star-crossed, but our present and future are filled with hope."

"OK, that is the most beautiful thing you've ever said," I said, leaning across the cards to kiss him, my lips lingering on his. Only a customer approaching had me remembering where I was. I sat back, and continued the reading. "The Tower is a card that warns that you are surrounded by chaos, but rather than the chaos leading to destruction, it means a change in the foundations of your life. But you must be honest with yourself, and not be a victim."

"You are the change," he said, nodding. "It makes sense."

I hesitated, looking down at the cards again. For the most part, they did make sense, but there was something about chaos being snuggled up against temptation that led to a little niggle of worry in the back of my mind. "Good. I have another half hour, but after that, we can talk about my boss and what we should do."

"I will patrol," he said, clutching his tablet as he gave over his seat to a giggling pair of young women. "Call me if you see ... *them*."

"Will do. Hi. Do you each want a reading, or a joint one?" I asked the girls.

The time passed quickly, and after I tallied up the takings, subtracted my share, and handed over the Faire's cut, it was past lunchtime.

"I'm starving," I told Ivo, and paused, looking at him.

"What?" he asked.

"You didn't ask for breakfast this morning. Aren't you hungry?"

"Yes, but I could not feed before you had a chance to do so." His eyes were serious, the gray a bit more pronounced than the green. I was puzzled by his ability to shift his eye color, and wondered if it had something to do with his emotions. I put a hand on his chest, about to tell him that I wasn't the one who had gone for more than eighty years without food, but at that moment, his eyes warmed and went mossy green with gray streaks. "Why are you making that face?" he asked.

"I'm a bit flabbergasted," I said, removing my hand. His eyes went gray green. I put my hand on his arm. His pupils flared and his irises headed straight for green. "OK, this is fun. Your eyes change color when I touch you."

"Beloved," he said in a tone that said much. "I am many things, but I am not a chameleon."

"I don't think they can actually change their iris colors." I glanced around, then moved in front of him, blocking the view of anyone around us, and placed my hand on his fly.

His eyes turned emerald green.

"Hoo!" I said, thrilled with this new power to gauge his emotions. "You're aroused."

"You have your hand on my rod," he said, his voice going a bit rough around the edges. "Of course I'm aroused. I do not, however, care for exhibitionism. If you wish to make love, we will return to the castle, and I will strip you and lick you from—"

"No," I said, laughing and kissing him to stop him from describing something I surely didn't want overheard by passing tourists.

He looked hurt.

"That is, yes, I want that, but not at this moment. For one, we both need food, and I want to talk about an idea I had while I was reading cards. Come on, I see a hamburger stand. I don't normally eat meat, but I'm going to have to keep my iron up if I want to get your gas tank back to full."

"If you're going to feed me, we will need to go back to the castle," he said.

I was about to ask him why, remembered what he'd told me about vamps and their Beloveds, and opted to get a to-go meal, which I planned to eat at the hotel.

"We'll both eat here, and then assuming you want me to stay with you, I'll check out," I told him a few minutes later when we entered the room.

No sooner had the door shut than he was scooping me up in his arms, heading straight for the bed.

"What—oh, lord, yes!" I said when he slid his hands up under my shirt, immediately possessing my breasts. I tossed my burger onto the nightstand, and gave myself up to the pleasure that was Ivo.

"This is … glorioski! Are you made of fire? This is really intense. Is sex with you always going to be like this?" I asked in between little panting gasps as Ivo slowly removed my leggings, his mouth moving along the exposed skin. He had slight stubble that made shivers of delight run down my spine while I pulled off the rest of my clothing.

He paused, his breath steaming a spot on my inner thigh, his eyes like liquid emerald. "Is it too much for you? Perhaps you should eat—"

"Are you kidding?" I wriggled my way out of my underwear, then more or less ripped his shirt off. "I don't want to do this on a full stomach. I can eat later, assuming you haven't melted all my innards into mush. Ivo! Your penis! It wasn't that big last night."

I swear he was about to roll his eyes as he shucked his shoes, pants, and underwear before returning to claim a spot between my legs. "I do not have a magical penis, Minerva. It is the same as it has always been—there when I need it, but otherwise not any different."

"Dude. You don't have to entertain that beast intimately. Oooh!" He nibbled the way up my leg to where said clearly defined space was anticipating his arrival with much celebrating. My toes curled with the sensation of his fingers as they stroked and teased and touched sensitive flesh while his tongue swirled and tormented, making me clutch the sheet beneath me as an orgasm started to build.

And then his mouth was on my thigh and pain stabbed like white heat for a second, before melting into rush of endorphins that pushed me closer to a climax. I stared down my body, amazed at the sight of his hair lying like silk on my flesh as he fed. For a second, a strange emotion swept over me, one of soul-deep satisfaction, a sense of rightness that mingled with erotic thoughts so heated I writhed in need. And then he was moving up my body, catching my legs over his arms, his body surging into me with deep, powerful thrusts.

I tried to say something, tried to tell him just how intensely wonderful the experience was, wanting him to know that I shared the sense of rightness in our joining, but my mind skittered away on waves of ecstasy.

I know, whispered in my mind.

The orgasm claimed my attention then, my body thrumming in time to the beating of his heart, his breath harsh against my neck as his hips went wild when he found his own moment of pleasure.

"Yep," I said a long time later. We were both lying flat on the bed, desperately trying to breathe, our bodies damp with our exertions.

Ivo tried to lift a hand from where it rested on his belly, but it fell back immediately. "What?"

"Yep, if this is going to be the standard level of lovemaking, then I'm going to have to take up a fitness routine. Because otherwise, I might die."

"You are immortal," he said. "Although you don't seem to heal like Dark Ones do."

I rolled onto my side, and kissed his bicep. "No, cartomancers are just your run-of-the-mill immortal. We know cards, and live a very long time unless someone lops off our heads or something like that, but we don't do the healing thing. And besides, that wasn't at all what I meant. I was giving you a compliment. It was a reflection on just studly you are. I'll say again—for a man who's been asleep for eighty-six years, you are really, really good at sex. Exceptionally good. Possibly godlike."

He looked pleased, but waved a hand in a vague gesture. "You helped some. You deserve a bit of the praise."

"Smart-ass," I said, pinching his arm before scooting up so I could lean against pillows. "Now that I can breathe again, do you mind if we pillow talk for a bit? I have a few things I want to talk about."

"You must eat." He looked with distaste at the bag holding my burger and fries. "You are hungry."

"Oh, yes, pass that over, please. Damn, I wish they'd had shakes. I would kill for a chocolate shake right now. I can pillow talk and eat at the same time. First, what did you think about the kidnappers?"

"I try not to think about them," he answered, lacing his

fingers beneath his head as I munched my way through my burger. "What did they say to you?"

"Nothing other than they were taking me to see Jason. What I want to know is why. It makes no sense, Ivo. They aren't working for him—they said they were hired by someone in Paris. I assume it was the shop owner from whom Jason stole the spell. So why are the baddies so hot and bothered about dragging me to a police station to see my boss?"

He was silent for a few minutes. "Could it be some sort of intimidation tactic?"

"Threatening to hand me over to the police, you mean?" I thought about that while consuming a few fries. "I don't see how it is supposed to scare me. I've already been grilled by them and released. They know I'm not the one who tried to abscond with the festival funds, and no one at the station mentioned a spell. I mean, they wouldn't, being mortal. No, something else is going on, and I want to know what."

"We will have to go see this employer of yours," Ivo said in a decisive tone, reaching for his clothing.

"I guess so, although from what I know of him, he doesn't seem to be too forthcoming with information. When do you want to go?"

He pulled on his shirt, frowning at the few spots where buttons had popped off when I ripped the shirt from him in my frenzy to get his naked body on mine. I grinned, and handed him the shirt I'd taken from his closet and had worn around my waist. "Is there anything wrong with now?"

"No, but you got red riding around in the sun." I gave him a quelling look that he avoided meeting. "When you weren't covered in road rash, that is. I assume the vampire lore is right in that you are sensitive to sunlight?"

"Somewhat. Those Dark Ones who have Joined with their Beloveds have more tolerance than others, but yes, in general I try to stay out of direct sunlight. Overcast days like today, however, pose even less of a threat than normal. We will go to the police station and see your employer."

"Not on your bike, we won't." Done eating, I went into the tiny bathroom and washed up, taking the opportunity to freshen up those parts of me that were still enjoying little aftershocks of tingling happiness.

"Finch has placed an automobile at my disposal," he told me, sitting on the edge of the bed, looking at something on his tablet.

I made a mental note to buy him the fanciest computer I could find. "Do you know how to drive?"

He reared back like I had insulted him. "Of course I do."

"Let me rephrase that—have you driven any car that was made after the year 1950?"

"Your point is invalid," he said, dismissing it with a little sniff that made me want to laugh. "I have driven an automobile before."

"I think maybe until we can find a nice big empty parking lot for you to have a refresher course, I'll take over driving duties," I said, gathering up my stuff, such as it was. "Come along, you handsome vampire, you. Let's go beard my boss in his police-laden den."

"Very well, but I'll have you know that I just looked up instructions on driving modern cars, and it says it's automatic. So I should be able to pilot the vehicle without any problem."

A half hour later, after spending the entire ride from Drahanská Castle to the police station trying to explain to Ivo the difference between manual and automatic transmission—and failing miserably, because I wasn't any too hip on the subject—we arrived at the police station, and I asked to see Jason.

It took another ten minutes while they checked to see if he was allowed visitors, and once they decided he was, they had to notify him that I was waiting.

We were finally escorted into a small interrogation room where Jason was handcuffed to a metal rail that ran along the top of the table, loudly bitching about his treatment. "I'll have my lawyers on you, see if I don't!" he shouted to a policewoman as she told us we had five minutes before she left the room.

"Hello, Jason," I said when he shouted something rude after the woman. "I see you are just as urbane as ever."

"It's about time you got your ass in here to help me," he snarled in response, turning bloodshot eyes on me. "Why has it taken so long for you to do your job? If you think I'm paying you for doing nothing but sitting around with your thumb up your ass, you can think again. Who's that?"

"Someone with a great deal more manners than you," Ivo said, holding a chair for me. "Beloved, would you like me to deal with this individual? I don't like you being exposed to such abuse."

"Beloved? Beloved?" Jason all but sneered the word, clearly about to make a snotty comment, but suddenly, he sat up straight and narrowed his eyes on Ivo. "Wait, you're a—"

"Boyfriend," I said quickly, glancing toward a camera that was perched at the ceiling level in the opposite corner. I had zero doubts that the room was under video surveillance. "He's my boyfriend."

"I believe 'fiancé' would be a more fitting word, since I am not a boy, but I will leave the matter for a more propitious moment," Ivo said in an even tone. I glanced at him. His eyes were dancing with amusement.

I melted inside.

Jason looked like he was going to argue, but I sat down and tapped on the table to distract him. "Why are two men who look like bulldogs in human form chasing me, Jason? Why did you tell them that I had a certain object you stole from a shop in Paris?"

It was Jason's turn to shoot a glance at the camera. "I didn't steal anything from Paris. I made a perfectly legal purchase of a medieval artifact. I can't be blamed if the shop owner did not understand digital currencies."

"Digital currency?" I asked. "What's that?"

"A decentralized currency that has no physical form. It's used by the elite," he answered in a lofty tone that I didn't for one minute believe.

"It sounds shady as hell. I mean, how can money be digital?"

"I don't have time to explain it to you." He looked petulant, and rattled the chain on his wrist restraints. "Now get me the fuck out of here."

I ignored his demand. "Why did you send the two big guys after me?"

His gaze flickered away. "I don't know what you're yammering on about. You're supposed to be working on getting me out. Did you call my lawyer like I asked? Did you even do that? I shouldn't be here. I did nothing wrong. I was set up. Someone made it look like I was trying to run off with the festival money. And you know what? The only person who would benefit in that case is you."

He's lying. The thought drifted through my head, but it felt somehow ... different. I rubbed the back of my neck, suddenly a bit weirded out.

"The two men that kidnapped me earlier today—you said that I had this artifact that you stole."

"Bought. I bought it. Legally."

I tapped on the table again, giving him a no-nonsense glare. "I can ask this as many times as it takes to get an answer: Why did you tell them that I have it?"

"What makes you think you don't?" he snarled, leaning forward in an obvious attempt to menace me.

Instantly, Ivo was on his feet jerking Jason back in his chair. "You will not threaten Minerva."

"Take your hands off me, you filthy bloodsucker!" Jason all but spat the words, little flecks of spittle on the corners of his mouth.

"It's all right," I told Ivo, tipping my head toward the chair next to me. "He can't do anything to us."

"He's lying," Ivo said, frowning, but he returned to stand behind me, obviously taking up a protective stance.

It warmed me to the tips of my toes. I'd never had anyone who sought to protect me.

I was not around whispered though my mind.

I shot a startled look over my shoulder at him, but just then Jason slammed down his fists on the table. "I hired you to help me. Why the hell aren't you doing that? This whole situation is bullshit. I'm not going to sit here and let you railroad me. Do something, you stupid woman!"

"OK. I will." I pulled out my tarot deck, which the police had let me bring with me into the interview room—after examining it to make sure that it didn't have any hidden razor blades or other forbidden substances—and gave it a quick shuffle.

"What are you doing?" Jason asked, sliding a quick glance toward the camera. A line of perspiration broke out on his forehead.

"Going to read what the universe has to say about your situation. How many times do you want me to cut it?"

"That's stupid," he said, licking his lips, his gaze flickering all around the room as if he was looking for an exit. "I told you when I hired you I don't like fortune-tellers."

"And I told you that cartomancy isn't fortune-telling. Ivo, would you cut the cards for Jason, since he seems disinclined to help?"

"I'm done here," Jason said, glancing toward the door. "I have better things to do than watch you do party tricks. Guard! I'm done!"

"Nine of staves," I said, laying down a card. "Oh, dear, are you having anxiety? Are you in mental distress? Because this card says you are your own worst enemy."

Jason licked his lips again, the perspiration growing. "Hello! Is anyone out there? I want to go back to my cell."

"Queen of swords." I gave him a long look. "There's a strong woman opposing you. One who, I should point out, doesn't tolerate fools gladly. She brings enlightenment where there is confusion."

Jason's gaze seemed glued to the cards even though he turned his face to call to the closed door. "Hey! Someone come and let me out!"

"Four of cups," I said. "Aww. This is another 'you're doing yourself in' card. This one says you're stuck due to a bad choice, and you're spinning your wheels. You have refused to take the way out of the situation because you just won't see the options available. Poor Jason."

I started pulling a fourth card, but at that part, he leaped to his feet, slamming his hands down on the table and yelling at the top of his lungs. "Let me out of here! You can't keep me here with this crazy woman and her fucking bloodsucker! They're going to attack me! Get me out! You have to protect me from them. It's a law!"

The policewoman hurried in at that point, scowling, but she got her keys out and unlocked Jason the whole time he was bitching about the Geneva Convention and being mistreated by everyone. He didn't once even look at me or Ivo before he was escorted out, still complaining loudly.

I stared at the open doorway through which he'd just passed, and slowly gathered up my cards before getting to my feet. "That was weird."

"Extremely so. Do you mind?" Ivo asked.

I handed him the three cards I'd picked up. "Not at all. Why do you think he looked so scared all of a sudden?"

He turned over the cards, narrowly examining them before giving them back. "I have no idea. Is there something about the cards that could so terrify him?"

"He was terrified, wasn't he?" I said, spreading the three cards before shaking my head. "Oddly so, but the answer is no. They're just cards, like I told you before. Bits of paper and ink. The magic comes from within me, not them."

"The meaning you gave them didn't seem to be distressing." He rubbed his chin, the slight sound of his whiskers rubbing against his fingers making a sensual shiver skitter down my back.

"They most definitely weren't. I just wish I knew what to

do about the two"—I glanced over toward the camera, and headed for the door—"guys."

"Don't worry about them," Ivo told me when we stopped to retrieve our belongings. "I will ensure your safety."

"This morning's kidnapping aside, I can take care of myself. I'm a big girl, you know," I told him, squeezing his arm nonetheless.

"You need not fear that I am in any way unaware of just how female you are," he said without looking at me, but a sudden flush washed up from my chest when extremely arousing images of our bodies entwined filled my head.

I was silent while we walked to our borrowed car, waiting until we were inside it before I asked Ivo, "This is going to sound crazy, but you do have any telepathic abilities?"

"Me?" His eyebrows rose. "No."

"Oh." I started the car, staring for a few seconds out the window, wondering if my mind was losing its grip on reality.

"Other than with my Beloved, of course," he added, then pulled out his tablet and tapped on it before shaking it, and tapping again. "This appears to be broken."

I stared at him. "What do you mean?"

He showed it to me. "I cannot connect to the Internet."

"No, not your tablet—and that's because you aren't connected to a network like you are within the range of Christian's castle. It has Wi-Fi. I meant what do you mean other than with your Beloved?"

"Wi-Fi," he repeated as if he was memorizing the word, nodding as he tucked the tablet away. "It needs a network. Of course. This fits in with what Finch told me. The Wi-Fi is not everywhere."

"No. Someday, perhaps, but not now. Ivo—"

"Dark Ones share a mark with their Beloved," he said, a little smile flirting with the corners of his lips, his eyes once again filled with amusement.

For some reason, the fact that he could have suffered for so long but still had a sense of humor warmed my heart. I knew then that I was a goner. I wasn't going to spend my life

with him in a mild form of lust and enjoyment of his pres-
ence—I was head over heels in love with him.

"That mark is the ability to read my mind?"

"More that we can share thoughts. I assumed, when you
did not respond to any of my attempts to reach you, that for
some reason we were denied that connection, but I take it
you have heard some of my comments to you?"

"I'm not sure," I said slowly. "Can you do it now? Or
does it have to be a special time?"

He was silent for a moment.

I shook my head. "Sorry, if you were broadcasting, my
receiver didn't pick up."

"Ah. Perhaps it is as I speculated, and we will simply not
be able to share that connection. It may be that by being so
long in the state of noctambul, I lost that ability." He took
my hand, his fingers warm on mine. "I will do what I can to
make up for that shortfall."

"You don't have to make up for anything," I told him,
leaning over to give him a kiss before pulling out onto the
street. "Where are we going?"

Ivo was silent for a few seconds before answering. "The
castle."

"To see your friends?" I asked. "Or to go to your room
and make hot, sweaty bunny love?"

He froze for a second, then slowly turned his head to
look at me with eyes that were a dark sage. "Is bunny love
some modern term for lovemaking so profound that you
won't be able to walk for at least three hours?"

"Oh, goddess, yes," I said, taking one hand off the steering wheel to fan myself. "Three hours, Ivo?"

"Possibly four if I get my second wind," he said, then
leaned back in the seat and closed his eyes.

But the smile on the corners of his lips was still there.

And my mind was filled with all sorts of thoughts that
had me rolling down the window on the drive back to his
temporary home.

SEVEN

"A cartomancer." Christian looked thoughtfully at Minerva when Ivo had explained the situation with her employer, in hopes that he might have a suggestion for ways to deal with the strongmen.

"I would simply remove them from her vicinity," Ivo had told them both when they settled into Christian's study. Minerva had chosen to sit on a leather love seat, which pleased Ivo since it allowed him to sit next to her in close contact. His arm was draped casually over her shoulders, and to his further delight, she leaned into him, placing a hand on his thigh. "But whoever sent those two might well send more."

Christian nodded, and then studied Minerva. "A cartomancer can do more than just read tarot cards, can they not?"

"Sure. Any cards will do," she answered. "Why?"

"You said that your employer had a strong reaction to them. Could it be something about the cards themselves that are problematic?"

"I doubt it." She gestured to where she'd set her deck of cards on a small table next to her. "They're just cards. I like these because of the pictures on them, but there's nothing special about them other than that. They're beat-up, and have been taped and glued back together over the years, but they're comfortable."

"Would you mind doing a reading for me?" Christian asked, looking inscrutable.

"Not at all." Minerva waited until Ivo pulled the table around to sit in front of her; then she shuffled and cut the deck several times before laying out five cards, and going through them while Christian watched closely.

Ivo heard nothing remarkable in the reading; it seemed to simply be a warning that he needed to practice patience, and that to rush forward into action would lead to folly—in other words, common sense—but when she was done, Christian nodded and gestured toward the cards.

"Do it again, please."

"Again?" Minerva gave a little shake of her head as she gathered up her cards and shuffled them. "I don't normally like to do that. Some people ask me to do a second reading if they don't like what I tell them, but—"

"Don't do a reading for me. Do one for yourself," Christian interrupted.

"Why her?" Ivo was driven to ask.

He felt mildly itchy that Christian thought he could give orders to his Beloved, but he reminded himself that not only was he a reasonable man without a shred of jealousy in his body; Minerva and he had sought out Christian's assistance.

But if Christian thought he could simply boss Minerva around, he would be forced to fisticuffs to show his host that only he had that right.

Hey!

Ivo glanced at Minerva, unsure of whether she'd actually spoken the protestation, or if he was so in tune with her that he imagined it, but she was frowning over her cards as she slowly cut them.

"The thief takers were after you. Your employer clearly has told someone that you have this spell that he stole. It was your cards that he was afraid of. All three events circle around you. I would like to know what you see in the cards regarding your situation."

She set down the cards. "I suppose I could, but I've never had much luck reading for myself. I think it's because I know these cards too well. They aren't strangers to me, if you will."

"Ah." Christian rose and returned with a deck of playing cards, which he handed to Minerva. "Will these better suit you?"

"Possibly, but this is one time when I can't promise you that I'll be any too accurate. Cartomancers often have blind spots when it comes to their own readings." She opened the pack and quickly discarded the two-through-six cards of each suit, then began to shuffle and cut the cards several times.

"Why have you removed those?" Ivo asked, touching the stack of rejected cards.

"Habit. It comes from the piquet deck. That was before your time, assuming you weren't around in the sixteenth century," she told him.

"I was born in 1832," he told her.

"I was around. I remember piquet well. It is a stripped deck," Christian said with a little nod.

"Right. Cartomancers read only the piquet decks, so that's what I do when I'm given a standard deck. OK, let's see what we have. I'll do a three-card spread, since I don't want to push my luck."

She flipped over three cards.

"Queen of spades, eight of spades, king of hearts," Ivo said, wondering if those were good or ill omens.

"Yeah." Minerva's expression was frozen as she looked first at the cards, then up to him. "I have to be honest, I've never had a reading like that for myself."

His arm tightened around her. "I will allow no harm to come to you."

"I appreciate that." She seemed to have difficulty swallowing for a second. "I expect you both want to know what they say."

"If it would not distress you too much," Christian said.

Her gaze dropped back to the cards. "It goes way past distressing, unfortunately. So, the queen of spades is a card that means imprisonment, or being bound to an extremely unfortunate situation. That might be tolerable, but then right next to it is the eight of spades."

"If this is too much for you—" Ivo started to say, his growing sense of unease pushing him to protect Minerva from whatever was troubling her. He just wanted to make things right so she would be happy and laughing, teasing him about his ability to pilot Christian's motorcycle.

"No, it's OK." She took a long intake of breath. "The eight of spades is a card of oppression. Destruction. Death, even. And also, imprisonment."

Silence filled the room.

"And the third card?" Christian asked.

Her lips twisted in a parody of a smile. "King of hearts. You'd think that would be good, but sadly, it's a card of slavery and bondage without end. So ... this is what the universe wants me to know about my life right now."

"Do it again," Ivo commanded, refusing to believe that his Beloved, his Minerva, whom he had found against all odds, and who now filled his heart and soul and mind, could have such a doomed future.

"I can't," she said, reaching for the cards, obviously about to gather them up.

"Wait," Christian said, tapping a finger on his lip. "The tarot reader at the GothFaire used to read for me. She drew something she called clarifying cards."

"Yes. Those are drawn when the message is confused or not obvious," Minerva said slowly.

"Would it be good to do one of those?" Ivo asked her.

"Possibly. Possibly not." Her eyes were dark with worry. He wanted nothing more than to take her to bed where he could make love to her and push all thoughts but those of pleasure from her mind, but he knew they would have no easy future together if they did not address this threat that hung over their heads.

"Do it," he told her, pulling her closer, relishing the feel of her warmth against his side.

She hesitated a second, then pulled the top card, and turned it over, gasping as she pressed into him. "King of spades. That's … it's a card of a man filled with hate. A powerful man."

"A devil," Christian said, his gaze on the card.

Minerva shuddered, and Ivo pulled her onto his lap, both arms around her as if he could protect her from the threats of the world. "We'll go away," he told her softly in her ear. "We'll find somewhere safe, and will remain there, away from the world. Away from this man of hate."

"Not a devil," Christian corrected himself. "*The* devil."

Ivo froze. "Demon lord?"

"I suspect so." Christian looked at Minerva. "Would your employer have the ability to steal a spell woven by a demon lord?"

"Oh goddess," she said, her fingers hard where they gripped Ivo's arm. "Not from the demon lord himself, but he could steal it from someone who possessed it. Are you thinking—"

"Bael," Christian said.

Ivo felt a protective surge that demanded he do something, anything, to protect his love. "Then we will find this spell and return it."

"Easier said than done. All my things except the clothes I was wearing yesterday, and my cards, are at the police station. They kept everything in case it was needed as evidence that I tried to abscond with the festival money," Minerva said, then to Ivo's dismay, pushed herself off him, and picked up another card, flipping it over. "Clarifying card: eight of clubs. Caution for a danger near at hand."

All three of them looked at Minerva's tarot cards sitting benignly next to the playing cards.

"It's something to do with the cards," Ivo said, trying to look at them from his peripheral vision.

"What are you doing?" she asked him.

"Ascertaining whether or not there's a curse on them. I don't see anything. Christian?"

He turned his head away from the cards, obviously doing the same thing. "No. No sign of a curse. Have you examined the cards themselves?"

"Not in so many words, but I've used them consistently for the last couple of days," Minerva answered, snatching up her cards as if he was about to take them. She fanned them out. "They're just cards. Nothing different about them. Nothing unusual."

"And yet, they held a secret so terrifying that your employer was sweating profusely to get out of the room," Ivo reminded her.

Minerva drew a sixth card from the stack of playing cards. "Clarification as to the threat: two of spades." She met his gaze, giving him a weak smile. "Destruction."

"A spell woven by Bael would be likely to be of such dire make," Christian agreed. "What we must do—"

The door was flung open, a swirl of wind accompanying the gesture sending the cards fluttering to the floor. Finch stood in the doorway, panting a little. He pinned Minerva back with a gaze that had the fine hairs on the back of Ivo's neck standing on end. "I don't know what the hell you've been doing, but there's four demons sniffing around the Faire. And in addition to that, a coven of warlocks has shown up claiming that they were summoned here to destroy a threat to the world. They riled up everyone there until they're all saying it's their duty to drive out the evil to save the world. Guess who they say is that threat?"

Minerva slumped in her chair. "Oh, goddess."

"What on earth did you do?" Finch asked, striding into the room.

"She did nothing," Ivo said, on his feet, filled with a desperate need to protect her. "She is innocent of all wrongdoing."

"That's not what the twelve warlocks are saying, and now several others are agreeing with them. I suspect it's the demons' influence. What's going on here? Are you playing cards?"

Christian quickly explained the situation while Ivo paced, his mind sorting through several options, then discarding them almost immediately.

"So you don't know what this spell is, or where it is, or even what effect it will have if someone finds it and casts it?" Finch asked in a tone with which Ivo took umbrage.

"It is not Minerva's fault. She did not steal the spell. She has nothing to do with it."

"Have you examined her cards?" Finch asked, nodding toward them.

"I've used them nonstop since Jason and I flew from Paris," she said wearily. "And both Ivo and Christian said they didn't see anything amiss with them."

Ivo wanted to wrap her in his arms and spirit her away to safety.

"May I see them?" Finch asked, holding out a hand.

"Who are these warlocks who are slandering Minerva?" Ivo demanded to know. He still felt itchy, as if he should be doing something, but he was at a loss as to what he could do other than go out and personally smite anyone who spoke ill of his Beloved. "Did the thief takers bring them to harass her in their stead? I will beat them to a pulp, individually or collectively."

Minerva's lips twitched. "You will?"

"Yes. They pose a threat to you."

"They also pose a threat to the rest of us, since the last I heard, they were threatening to storm the castle to make Minerva come out and face them." Finch took the cards that Minerva gave him, and began to examine them closely.

Christian sighed heavily. "And here was I thinking the days of mortals storming my home with pitchforks and torches were long gone."

"They would hardly do that," Ivo told him. "It's not as if you are living in the pages of a gothic novel, after all. At best, they would merely make nuisances of themselves as they did with my mausoleum."

Eve, the housekeeper whom Ivo had met when he arrived eighty-six years before, opened the door to the study and gave Minerva a long look before she announced, "There are people at the front entrance. They are armed with burning torches, and demand that you turn over to them the woman who bears a spell intended on destroying them all. I have been informed that if she does not come out, they will set fire to the castle."

Christian cocked an eyebrow at Ivo, who felt a rising sense of frustration with the whole situation.

"Evidently, I am wrong," he managed to say, wrapping himself in the dignity that came to all Dark Ones.

"Oh, goddess," Minerva said, her elbows on her legs as she leaned her head into her hands. "Now we're living through a Frankenstein movie. And it's all my fault."

"It is not your fault," Ivo said, moving immediately to her side. "You are not responsible for either your employer's actions or those of the two strongmen, who have obviously stirred the crowd to do their dirty work. You are blameless in this whole situation. Blameless and uninvolved except in the most tangential manner."

"Blameless, maybe, but I am not so sure she's uninvolved," Finch said, frowning over a card. He held it up to the light. They all looked at it.

"It's just a card," Ivo said. "Somewhat tattered."

Minerva craned to look. "The Hanged Man? Yeah, that got wet and the front lamination started coming off, so I had to glue it back down. That's why it's a bit lumpy."

"Is it?" Finch slid his fingernail along the edge of it. Christian, who had gone to look out a window that faced the front entrance, moved over to where Finch was bent over the card. He pursed his lips, went to his desk, and returned with a long, wickedly sharp letter opener, which he handed to Finch. The latter applied it to the edge of the card, looking up to add, "Or is it *this* that is making it thicker?"

They all stared when he spread his hands, revealing two cards. The first was the Hanged Man card, but the second, the Sun card, was torn along the perimeter where Finch had separated the cards, obviously glued together. In the dead center of the card, a tiny scrap of vellum resided, minute text written in a dirty brown ink, the writing so small as to almost be illegible.

Almost.

"Holy shiznits," Minerva said, her mouth an O as she moved to Ivo's side. "There really was something in my cards. Literally in them. Wow. Is that—"

"Don't touch it," Ivo warned, taking her hand when she reached out to poke at the bit of vellum. He met first Finch's, then Christian's gaze. They both nodded. "My medieval Latin may not be as strong as I would like, but it's clear from the first line that this was, indeed, a spell created by the premiere prince of Abaddon, Bael."

"The head honcho of hell wrote that?" Minerva's eyes were huge when she watched while Christian, carefully taking the Sun card from Finch, walked over to his desk, where he rummaged around until he extracted a small wooden box, from which he dumped a number of pen nibs. Tipping the card, the vellum slid into the box.

Everyone breathed in relief when he closed the lid, snapping shut a latch.

"What did the spell say?" Minerva asked.

"It was a destructive spell to destroy enemies of the bearer, from what I saw," Christian said, glancing at Ivo, who nodded.

"It most definitely should not be made available to anyone but the most cautious and respectful of collectors," Ivo said.

"Well, that answers the question of why Minerva was the target of the thief takers," Finch said, then cocked his head when the pounding of someone at the front doors echoed throughout the castle. "Who is going to tell them?"

"I will," Ivo said, straightening his shoulders, and would have marched out to inform the crowd they must disperse or face his wrath, but Minerva stopped him.

"That is insanely brave of you," she told him, kissing his

chin. "With an emphasis on the word *insane*, but you get bonus points for the brave side."

"I will not allow anyone to harm you. Not only because it would make you unhappy, but because you are my Beloved. It is my role to defend you," he told her, gently releasing himself from the hold she had on his arm. "Now stay back, and allow me to commence smiting those who refuse to be reasonable."

"Are all vampires like this?" she asked Christian.

"Dark Ones," Finch murmured as Christian answered, "Yes. It is the way of things. Although perhaps not all Dark Ones are quite so determined to get themselves killed as is Ivo. Let us think for a moment before we act."

Ivo was halfway down the hall when the others caught up to him, Minerva throwing herself in front of him to stop him. "Hang on, Ivo. You don't have to go Terminator on everyone. Christian has a cat-caught-at-the-cream-bowl look that says he probably has an idea."

"I would object to the comparison, but as time is of the essence, I will simply say that, yes, I do have an idea. The crowd is here for what purpose?"

Several deep banging noises emerged from the two front doors, right on cue.

"They want Minerva," Finch said.

"They can't have her," Ivo said in a near growl, for the first time in his life considering the act of punching his friend in the face.

"They want the spell," Christian corrected. "So I say we give it to them."

"Are you insane?" Minerva asked him.

"Beloved, please. Let me handle this," Ivo told her.

"Excuse me? Did you just tell me I couldn't speak? Because if you did, I'm going to sock you in the gooch."

Ivo narrowed his eyes at the unfamiliar term. "Where—"

"Your crotch," she said with what he felt was a far too pointed look at his fly. "And for the record, I don't want to punch you there, because I want those parts hale and hearty later on. I have plans for them. *Sexy* plans."

He resisted the urge to cover his privates with a hand, and instead gave her a firm look. "I am the Dark One. You will allow me to deal with others of my kind."

"There's an angry mob at the door, a curse by the actual leader of hell in the box that Christian is holding, and you want to stop for an exercise in protocol?" She took a deep breath, then, to Ivo's surprise, made a deep bow as she swept a hand toward Christian. "By all means, be my guest. Deal with your fellow vamps."

"Dark Ones," Ivo corrected automatically, then turned to Christian and said, "Are you insane?"

"Dude!" Minerva said, and punched him in the arm.

Absently, he rubbed the spot as he continued. "You can't give a spell of such power to a mob."

"I have no intention of doing so," Christian said, and gestured toward the stairs. "Come, there is a balcony on the second floor. We will go out there to speak to the mob that your Beloved has stirred up."

"I'm not above punching your gooch, either," Minerva told Christian as Ivo escorted her up the stairs.

"About that, I have no doubt," he told her. Ivo cast a glance over his shoulder at Christian and Finch, but the latter merely looked annoyed, while Christian appeared to be amused.

He smiled at Minerva, who did a double take. "What?" she asked in a whisper as they reached the top of the stairs, and Christian moved past them to show them how to access the balcony.

"You threatened Christian. He is a very old Dark One. He has much gravitas. He is much respected."

"Yeah, well, he's also flipping me shit, and I don't tolerate that from anyone."

"I would have defended your honor," Ivo protested.

"Of course you would. I don't doubt that at all. But as I said before, I'm not a wimp who can't fight her own battles. Well, some of them. For most of them, I would like your help."

"We will fight together," he said, the feeling of happiness flooding him. He had always had a vague notion of what it would mean to find a Beloved, but nothing had prepared him for the sense of joy that wrapped around him.

He began to mentally write a few lines of praise to Minerva's shining spirit, which had turned his life from desolation to happiness.

"What are you muttering about?" Finch asked a moment later.

He paused, his eyes on Minerva, wondering if she would ever know just how much he loved her. "I was trying to find a rhyme for vulva."

"You what?" Finch asked, clearly appalled.

Ivo patted him on the arm, appreciating the fact that Finch had his best interests at heart. "You're right, of course."

"I should hope so."

They followed after Minerva and Christian.

"A rhyme isn't at all necessary. Blank verse is entirely suitable for an ode to her vagina. I'm thinking of calling it 'Midnight in the Lady Garden of Good and Even Better.' Minerva will appreciate the care I took with the title."

Finch choked, and it took several minutes of patting him on the back before they could enter the upper gallery that led to the balcony.

EIGHT

"Wow. I don't think I've ever actually seen an angry, torch-toting mob before," I said when Christian and I stood on the stone balcony that sat above the big double doors leading into his castle.

"Unfortunately, I cannot say the same." He turned back, looking for Ivo and Finch, who arrived a minute later, the latter with a face that was beet red, his eyes and nose streaming. "Problems, Finch?"

"No." He slid Ivo a glance, then said softly, "I'll tell you later."

I wondered what that was about, but before I could ask Ivo, someone in the crowd had evidently heard us, because a few people backed up, craned their heads to see us, then started shouting and waving their torches.

The crowd roared and started calling too many things for me to understand.

"Whoa! Can just one person at a time speak?" I yelled, moving to the front of the balcony, figuring that since it was my blood they were evidently after, I would speak for Team Vampire.

I'd reckoned without Mr. Protective, however. Ivo moved to my side, and with a glare that took in the whole of the thirty or so people gathered outside Christian's front door, he wrapped an arm around me in a clearly possessive move.

"You heard Minerva. Pick a spokesperson," he said with a voice that dripped with authority.

I had been about to protest both his gesture and what I assumed would be his attempt to take over control of the situation, but he did neither.

Immediately, the people began to squabble amongst themselves as to who was going to speak for them.

"You're not going to lay down some misguided archaic line about me standing back and letting you handle this?" I asked Ivo.

He looked genuinely surprised, his eyebrows rising, then falling back to their normal position. "No. Did you wish for me to do so? I am happy to oblige you, but I assumed that since this concerns your cards and your employer, you would wish to be the one leading the proceedings."

I licked the tip of his nose. "If I wasn't already in love with you, that would have done the trick."

"You love me?" A variety of emotions passed over his face: astonishment, gratitude, a smug male cockiness, and, finally, a look so steamy, I wanted to tear off his clothes and molest him on the spot.

I see nothing wrong with this plan.

"Ivo! I heard you!" I said on a gasp, clutching his shirt with both hands.

"I heard him, too, which is a miracle considering just how loud those people are being," Finch said, peering down at them. "You'd think they could pick a spokesperson without resorting to beating each other over the head with the torches."

I ignored the fact that three men who were wearing what I thought of as LARP-standard wizard wear, with long gowns, leather gauntlets, and wooden staves, were now rolling around on the ground beating up one another, while the others stood in a circle around them, egging them on.

Only the two thief takers, who stood in the back, their massive arms crossed over their beefy chests, ignored the hullabaloo to stare at the balcony where we stood.

"You love me? You really love me?" Ivo asked, his gaze searching mine.

"Yes, but I—"

"Minerva, cartomancer, come forward!" a woman's voice called from below.

"Later," I told Ivo, giving him a swift kiss. "We'll talk about this later."

"As well as physical forms of demonstration. Don't forget about those," he said.

I stepped up to the edge of the balcony, the stone balustrade cold beneath my fingers. "I am Minerva. Who speaks?"

"I am Wanda, Gary the Gray's wife." The woman made a face, then jerked her thumb over her shoulder. "That's Gary back there with the broken collarbone. He can't speak without whining, so I'm here to do the job for him."

Behind her, the three men who had been fighting were now separated and sitting on the ground with a few people around them, obviously tending to their wounds. The others were clustered around the woman named Wanda, who had a baby carrier strapped to her front, a little knit cap visible over the top of it indicating she had her child with her.

"Hello, Wanda. This is Ivo. He's my boyfriend," I said, gesturing toward Ivo.

"Fiancé," he corrected.

"Mazel tov," she said.

"Thank you. And this is Christian Dante, who owns the castle that you guys are trying to break into, and can I say that I'm sure he doesn't appreciate anyone doing damage to the building or grounds, so the two of you who are rolling around in the flower bed, if you could go do that somewhere else, I have no doubt Christian would be grateful."

The two men who were, in fact, locked in an amorous display, clambered out of the bed of late-blooming dahlias, and had the grace to look embarrassed. "Sorry," one of them called up to Christian. "We're celebrating our anniversary and got a bit carried away."

Christian inclined his head, but I heard him sigh to himself.

"And this is Christian's nephew Finch."

A cheer went up.

Finch lifted his hand in acknowledgment.

Ivo and I stared at him.

Finch gave a half shrug. "I stood a few rounds at the local pub. It was excellent research for my book."

"So now that we have all the introductions, what is it you guys want?" I called down.

"The spell that you intend to use on all of us!" One of the men in a wizard gown started forward, but two others pulled him back.

"We heard that you might have a spell of untold power," Wanda said somewhat apologetically, rocking from side to side now and rubbing the back of the baby carrier. "And those never end up well, do they, ladies?"

Four other women had gathered behind her, and they all nodded.

"So we wanted to find out first whether or not you do have it."

I looked at Christian.

He sighed again, but handed me the small wooden box. I held it up. "I do."

Pandemonium broke out in the crowd until Wanda and her gang of four turned and yelled at everyone to stop the noise, or there would be hell to pay when they got back home. The assorted men and women settled down again.

"I should add that we only just discovered the spell hidden in one of my possessions. None of us knew it was there."

"A likely story," someone shouted from the back. It was one of the thief takers.

"And are you willing to hand it over to us?" Wanda asked.

"Are you kidding?" I asked.

Wanda smiled. "I thought it was worth asking. Very well, we agree that it would be as much a folly for one of us to have so much power on tap as you, so we'd like to request that you destroy the spell. We realize that you won't wish to do so, but we've prepared a statement with several bullet points as to the wisdom of taking that course. Carolina, do you have the list?"

One of the women in the back pushed her way forward, waving a flyer from the battle of the bands. "Here it is."

"Excellent." Wanda consulted the list. "Point one: it is a dangerous spell, and might be subject to being stolen by an unscrupulous person. Point two—"

"You know, as much as I love a good bulleted list, we don't need to hear more. None of us want the spell. We're not demon-lord-spell sorts of people. We're happy to destroy it," I called down.

"Well … ," Christian started to say, but stopped when Ivo glared at him.

"What's the best way to destroy a spell?" I asked the love of my life when the crowd broke out into several shouts of approval.

"Burn it?" Ivo said, glancing at the others.

"I would say that's the best method," Christian answered.

"We're going to burn it, OK?" I asked the women.

"With all due respect," Wanda said after a minute, when two of the women consulted with her, "we'd like to see you do it. Just so everyone can make sure it's gone, and we can get back. I need to pump like something crazy since Janet here didn't want to switch nipples for dinner."

"Do we have a lighter—ah. Thank you. Um."

"Would you like me to do it?" Ivo asked.

"You light it, and I'll hold it until the fire is too close to my fingers," I instructed, and opened the box.

A hush fell on the crowd, even the three wizards who had fought one another now quiet. Gingerly, I picked up the bit of vellum by the corner that was free from any writing, holding it up for the people to see.

There were a number of *ooohs* and *aaahs*; then I held it over the open box, and nodded at Ivo. "Go ahead."

He flicked the lighter a few times until he got a flame that wobbled in the slight breeze, cupping his hand around it as he held it to the opposite edge. It took a few seconds before the vellum caught on fire, but almost immediately I noticed two things: the first was a horrible oily black smoke that billowed off the scrap and immediately wrapped around my wrist, and the other was that faint red symbols were visible for a second in the smoke.

"Drop it!" Ivo commanded, his voice hard as stone.

Surprised by the vehemence, I did as he ordered, letting the spell fall into the box. He slammed the lid closed on it.

"Why did you do that?" I whispered, glancing worriedly at the crowd. "It won't be able to burn in there."

"Didn't you see the symbols? The spell almost touched you. If it had done so, you would have been its new receptacle."

The people below us looked puzzled for a moment; then a few gave a feeble cheer.

"That's it!" I called to them, and, holding my hand strategically so as to hide the half-burned bit of vellum, displayed the interior of the box. "It's gone."

"Well, that's a relief. Now I can go pump. Come along, Gary. We'll see to your collarbone back in town," Wanda told her husband, who was listing heavily to one side.

The rest of the people seemed disinclined to leave, their torches wavering as they hesitated to follow Wanda and her hurt wizard.

At least they hesitated until Finch called out, "Shall we move this gathering to the Flogged Bishop? First round is on me!" The torches were raised high in tribute before there was a general stampede down the road toward the town.

"What are we going to do?" I asked Ivo, who had taken the box from me and was studying the bit of vellum.

"It'll have to be destroyed. It's too powerful to remain as is."

"Perhaps if we use some sort of tongs to hold it?" Finch suggested.

"We can try that," Christian agreed, and disappeared inside only to return a few seconds later with fireplace tongs, which he handed to Ivo.

"I'll hold it this time," he told me. "You light it."

"Are you being brave, protective, or thoughtful?" I asked, taking the lighter from him.

"All three?" he asked.

"That's going to earn you bonus forms of physical demonstrations of just how much I love you. Go on, my brave poet. Burn that sucker up so we can go to your room and do an untold number of carnal things to each other."

He managed to get the scrap clutched by the wrought iron of the fireplace tongs, and held it out for me. I lit it, then stepped back when he gestured me away.

"Just in case the smoke goes for you—shit!"

The scrap began to spew the same dense black smoke as when I'd held it, immediately twisting its way up the tongs, but before Ivo could drop it, it had reached his hand, encasing it in a solid black mass, little red symbols flashing within it for a second.

"Ivo are you—no!" I stared in horror as the black smoke began to peel away from his hand. "Oh, goddess, no!"

Ivo, who had been staring with what I could only assume was the same expression that I wore, looked at his hand, which was still in a position as if it was holding the tongs. Only his hand from the wrist down was black, completely black, as if it had been dipped in the densest coal.

"Call a healer," Christian ordered Finch, who pulled out his phone.

"I'm a doctor," I told him absently, then asked Ivo, "Does it hurt?"

"No. It doesn't feel like anything." Ivo lifted his arm, closely examining his hand. "It feels like it's not even there. Like it's dead or—"

His hand broke off at the wrist, and fell to the stone floor of the balcony, shattering into a dozen pieces.

I felt a growing need to scream. Panic caught me by the throat as I looked first from the smashed hand to the man who meant everything to me. Automatically, I had braced myself for the gore that accompanied the loss of a limb, but there was none. The end of Ivo's wrist was covered in skin, just as if it had instantly healed over.

"What the hell?" I asked, realizing my voice was rising in panic. I clutched Ivo's uninjured arm, searching his face for signs of distress, but there were none. He looked as stunned as I felt. "Let's get you inside. Goddess—I don't know what happened, but you need to sit down. Why is there no blood? Vampires bleed. I know you do. I saw you bleed all over in France."

"I think it was the spell," he said, turning his wrist first one way, then the other while he examined it. "It clung to my hand, and destroyed it when it was itself destroyed."

"Your hand!" I said on a near wail. "Your lovely long-fingered hand! Holy shit, Ivo!"

"I have another," he said, waggling his free hand at me.

"Am I insane, or are all of you?" I asked the three men, turning to look at the other two, both of whom wore thoughtful expressions. "Why is no one making a big deal out of this? Ivo's hand just fell off. It fell off. It's gone. It's toast."

"That's quite evident," Finch said, a little frown pulling his brows together. "But since Ivo doesn't seem to be in any distress, and the spell has been destroyed, I would say that all's well that ends well."

"All's well?" I said, my voice rising as I turned to face him. *"All's well?"*

"All is definitely not well," a deep voice said from inside. The thief takers moved out onto the balcony, nudging first the crumbled ashes of the vellum, then the black broken pieces of Ivo's fingers. "Not well at all. Our client will be most displeased that the spell is no more."

"Displeased," the second one repeated, then suddenly looked hopeful. "Still, he can't blame us for it, can he? What's done is done, say I. Let's go get some food. That bloodsucker there said he's paying for the first round."

Finch looked like he wanted to protest, but I was too focused on Ivo to care.

"My darling. My love. What can I do for you?" I asked, desperate to help him in his time of need. "I am not terribly learned in Dark One medical care, so we can get a healer familiar with your kind if you like. Maybe we can reattach your hand—"

A crushing noise of someone stepping on incinerated fingers had me flinching and glaring at the nearest thief taker, who bared his teeth in what I assumed was meant to be a smile.

"Sorry," he said, and carefully scraped the pulverized remains of the fingers onto a bit of stone on the balustrade. Christian hustled the two men out of the castle.

"I give up," I said, wanting to scream and cry and do something for Ivo. The problem was, I didn't know what he wanted.

You. I want you.

I can hear you again! I said, goose bumps rippling down my arm. *In my head, I can hear you, just like I did a little bit ago.*

Excellent, he said. I had the sense of satisfaction filling him. *I wondered if it would come when you redeemed my soul.*

"Your what, now?" I asked.

"Soul. I was born of an unredeemed Dark One; thus I was the same. Until you. Now that you are here, I am whole."

I looked pointedly at his wrist.

"Well, mostly whole."

"I have a friend who is big into electronics," Finch said, tugging on his earlobe. "I wonder if he couldn't rig up some sort of prosthetic high-tech hand for you, Ivo. One that would allow you do things."

"What sort of things?" I asked, taking Ivo's good arm and gently steering him inside. I had a need to get him into his room, not so I could molest him, but to make sure he was not hiding hurt from me.

That's a shame. I could do with the molesting.

OK, this is going to take a bit of getting used to, I told him.

"Things he'd do with his left hand," Finch said, following us. "Holding things. Using tools. Driving my uncle's motorcycle."

"Piloting the machine!" Ivo said, his eyes lighting up with joy despite the situation.

I marveled at him, amazed he could be so happy given the fact that he'd just lost a hand.

Sweet, you are worth infinitely more to me than a mere hand. You are my sun. My stars. My moon. I have composed a few lines that I think will express just how much you mean to me. Shall I recite them to you?

"Yes," I said, laughing despite the horrible events of the last few minutes. "Go ahead, and recite away. And after that, I'm going to carefully, very carefully make love to you. Because you are the most amazing man, and I need to show you in a very tangible way just how glad I am that fate sent you into my life."

"That's completely illogical. Beloveds and Dark Ones are made for each other. There's no matter of fate involved," Finch said with a hint of an eye roll, and took himself off to the pub, where no doubt he would end up paying a small fortune.

"Don't listen to him," Ivo told me, opening the door to his room with a grand gesture. "He's jaded. Always has been."

"He'll feel differently when he finds his Beloved," I told the love of my life, my heart so full I wanted to sing.

"I doubt if he has one. His parents were Joined when he was born, so he doesn't need one to save him, the way you did me. Now, if you would make yourself comfortable on the bed, I will recite for you a poem I call 'Minerva, Goddess of Wisdom Who Has Claimed My Heart and Makes My Loins Throb in a Manner Wholly Unconnected with Infection or Disease.' Ready?"

I giggled as I took a seat on the bed, thanking the fates for setting my path to cross Ivo's a second time. *I'm ready, my sweet, adorable vampire.*

Dark One. "'O Minerva, goddess with the shining breasts that fit so perfectly in my hands, your spirit has claimed mine just as I have claimed your thighs, and ne'er shall we be parted, unlike your luscious previously aforementioned thighs …'"

It was a *very* long poem.

EPILOGUE

To: Finch (justfinch@aol.com)
From: Ivo (masterpoet@aol.com)

Finch, Minerva has asked me to let you know that we are settled in a house in British Columbia, Canada. She grew up here, and claims I will like it because it rains quite a bit. She doesn't understand that I don't care where we live, since anywhere would be a home so long as she is present, although I admit the gloomy, damp skies are strangely pleasing to my newly found soul.

You really must look into finding a Beloved, even though you don't strictly need one. It is very satisfying. On many levels.

How is your book going? Did Christian get his mausoleum fixed once the Faire and accompanying festival left? It was very kind of him to offer us his machine, but Minerva has promised us that we will learn how to pilot two of our own, once she has ascertained a person to provide necessary lessons. We both know that such things are not needed on my part, but she is adamant that we can't have a license to pilot the motorcycles unless we have training, and I am loath to ruin anything she has her heart set on.

Did you ever receive confirmation of your uncle's suspicions that it was Bael himself who sent the thief takers to look for his spell? I hesitate to tell Minerva that such a being was behind the attack on her, but I would like to know. Regardless, I am most vigilant in making sure no one else seeks to find her.

Minerva has reminded me to thank you for the news of her ex-employer, and her things, which we received yesterday. She is particularly glad that the police have committed to charging him for the embezzlement, although given that he was obviously terrified upon hearing that demons had been sent to find him, I suspect he will consider himself luckier to be in prison than out in the world where Bael could take repercussions on him.

I am also to pass along thanks to your uncle for his invitation to visit when GothFaire and the festival return next year. I would not hesitate to commit us to attending, but Minerva thinks it would be a good opportunity for me to join a local college, for as she says, one is never too old to learn. Naturally, she intends for me to teach poetry and related subjects, not attend classes themselves. I have considered her proposal, and think it has much merit. I am in the process of composing a few lines to tell her the good news.

Do not hesitate to visit us when you next come to Canada. We would be delighted to have you stay with us as long as you like, and of course, the offer extends to your uncle, should he wish to head to this side of the world.

I am truly grateful for everything that you both have done for me. You are the truest of friends, and I count myself infinitely lucky to have had you to watch over me until such time as Minerva found me again.

Ah. Minerva has just placed before me a catalog of offerings by the local college, and she's circled a class on writing poetry that she said would be perfect for me. I shall study the synopsis, but I'm sure that I will have no problem in working up my own syllabus for a master class. There are few poets who have been writing as long as I have, after all.

My best wishes to you and Christian.

Ivo (and Minerva)

NOTE TO READERS

My lovely one! I hope you enjoyed reading this book, which I handcrafted from the finest artisanal words just for you. If you are one of the folks who likes to review books, I'd love it if you posted a review for it on your favorite book spot (be sure to tell me if you do, so that I can lavish praise all over you).

If you're looking for some fun behind-the-scenes tidbits and exclusive material available free just for you via Book-funnel, hie thee over to my website at katiemacalister.com and sign up for the newsletter.

Did you enjoy the tale of Ivo and Minerva? Want more vamps? Luckily, I have more!

Here's a reading list, arranged chronologically by story:

UNLEASHED (novella) [Also in A FISTFUL OF VAMPIRES anthology]
IN THE COMPANY OF VAMPIRES
CONFESSIONS OF A VAMPIRE'S GIRLFRIEND
MUCH ADO ABOUT VAMPIRES
A TALE OF TWO VAMPIRES
THE UNDEAD IN MY BED (novella)
THE VAMPIRE ALWAYS RISES
ENTHRALLED

ABOUT THE AUTHOR

For as long as she can remember, Katie MacAlister has loved reading. Growing up in a family where a weekly visit to the library was a given, Katie spent much of her time with her nose buried in a book.

Two years after she started writing novels, Katie sold her first romance, *Noble Intentions*. More than seventy books later, her novels have been translated into numerous languages, been recorded as audiobooks, received several awards, and have been regulars on the *New York Times, USA Today, Publishers Weekly*, and *Wall Street Journal* bestseller lists. Katie lives in the Pacific Northwest with two dogs, and can often be found lurking around online.

You are welcome to join Katie's official discussion group on Facebook, as well as connect with her via TikTok and Instagram. For more information, visit her website at www.katiemacalister.com

CPSIA information can be obtained
at www.ICGtesting.com
Printed in the USA
BVHW041950230223
659117BV00007B/50

9 781952 737657